JANE AUSTEN, ACTION FIGURE AND OTHER PLAYS

by

Elaine Avila

NoPassport Press
Dreaming the Americas Series

Jane Austen, Action Figure; At Water's Edge; Burn Gloom: Rituals on Millennium Eve; Quality: the Shoe Play
Copyright 2012 by Elaine Avila.

All rights reserved. Except for brief passages quoted in newspaper, magazine, radio, or television reviews, no part of this book may be reproduced in any form or by any means, electronic or mechanical, without permission in writing from the author. Professionals and amateurs are herby warned that this material, being fully protected under the Copyright Laws of the United States of America and of all the other countries of the Berne and Universal Copyright Conventions, is subject to royalty. All rights including, but not limited to professional, amateur, recording, motion picture, recitation, lecturing, public reading, radio and television broadcasting, and the rights of translation into foreign languages are expressly reserved. Particular emphasis is placed on the question of readings and all uses of these plays by educational institutions, permission for which must be secured from the author.
For all rights, including amateur and stock performances, contact the author Elaine Avila, avilaelaine@yahoo.com or her representation: The Playwrights Guild of Canada, 215 Spadina Ave., Suite #210, Toronto, Ontario, Canada, M5T 2C7, telephone: 416.703.0201 fax: 416.703.0059, General Inquiries: info@playwrightsguild.ca

Book Design: Caridad Svich

Artwork for the cover:
Photo: "Casco Viejo, Panamá City" by Elaine Avila
Graphic Design by Winona Avila

NoPassport Press: Dreaming the Americas Series
First edition 2012 by NoPassport Press
PO Box 1786, South Gate, CA 90280 USA;
NoPassportPress@aol.com
ISBN: 978-0-578-10420-1

Clara Tristan as Susie, Myrna Castro as Emily Dickinson in
<u>*Jane Austen, la Figura de Acción*</u>,
Teatro Lagartija, Panamá City, Panamá, directed by
Ted Gregory
photo: Ted Gregory, courtesy of ELATE (Educational Latin American Theatre Exchange)

Para o meu Pai e a minha Mãe. Beijinhos.

TABLE OF CONTENTS

"Pushing Buttons in Panamá,"
Forward by Ted Gregory

<u>The Plays:</u>

Jane Austen, Action Figure

Quality: the Shoe Play

At Water's Edge

Burn Gloom

Afterword by Kathleen Weiss

PUSHING BUTTONS IN PANAMÁ

PANAMANIAN ACTRESS
(whispers)
Esto es escritura valiente.
INTERPRETER
(loud and clear)
This is brave writing!
(the actress smiles with a slight hint of embarrassment)

  Although my Spanish is ok, I didn't need an interpreter to sense what this actress had experienced. She had just read a scene from Elaine Avila's, *Jane Austen: Action Figure and other short plays*, in a new translation by Myrna Castro. Emily Dickinson has been ripped from the arms of her lover who, dressed in her wedding gown, is on her way to marry Emily's brother. As the lover is being led off to the sound of wedding bells, Emily drowns them out in one final plea, "I'll look out my window and see your windows. Glass. Certain slants of light. Is this all I am to have, the pain of knowing my brother is nestled 'gainst your breast? Susie, see my body—touch me--".
  This was Panamá, steeped in tradition and struggling with progress – the bridge of the Americas. Marriage is sacred here and homosexuality has only been legal for maybe 10 years. And we were heading into rehearsals for *Jane Austen: la Figura de Acción y otros obras cortas* (JAAF), which will have its world premiere at the International Festival de Cocos. Sexuality and gender roles are about to be explored, motherhood questioned, men were to play little girls and women were to play men, our sides were about to ache from that special kind of hysterical laughter that accompanies audacity, and traditional theatrical structure was going to be subjugated to surprise and possibility. In short – we were about to

be kicked in the guts. And we were in Panamá. What were we thinking? We were at a crossroads – both literally and metaphorically. This was a play about Jane Austen, a superwoman among writers – it was brave, bold, and required no less from all collaborators. We were up to the challenge – as a director this is what sustains me. This is Elaine Avila writing.

"So...what type of play is *Jane Austen: la Figura de Acción?*" a local radio host asks. I could tell from his expression that perhaps he was looking from something more astute than the response I gave him. "Well...it's a funny play." I really do hate to categorize new work in terms of genre or style. Is this necessary anymore? This seems to be an archaic practice from a pre-globalized time. Maybe that's the problem – theatre hasn't gone global yet, not really. Try explaining the significance of Tennessee Williams as poetic realism to a group of poet/playwrights from Latin America and you will quickly realize the absurd futility of it all. In a capacious discipline why we continue to box artists into specific corners baffles me. I am a white male director from the Midwest directing a new Spanish translation of a play that challenges gender roles written by a female playwright currently teaching in New Mexico and performed by Spanish speaking actors in a staunchly traditional, historically war torn country in Central America. Now... explain that! How does this happen? It just does. It's possible and it's real – it's happening.

That said, I love writers who explore limitless possibilities. Elaine's writing is as naturalistic as two life-long lovers recalling seemingly insignificant but oh so precious moments from their past needs to be. It is as experimental as conjuring the spirit of Jackie Kennedy through a shoe requires. Ultimately, genre and style be damned, her characters say what they need to say. No more, no less. If the rules of the world they live in sometimes need to bend to accommodate the force of their desires, so be it. There is a master of the craft at work here in these plays – there is an artist respecting her impulses – the writing is at once specific and limitless.

    When I first arrived in Panamá as a Fulbright Scholar in 2010, invited to help establish the first MFA theatre program in Latin America, it soon became evident that I was to spend the next year in a land of contradictions. Panamá City with its towering Miami meets Las Vegas skyline is a cosmopolitan city with a clear international presence. Yet, just a short distance into the interior away from the city center, you can find the largest rainforest outside of the Amazon Basin. In the shadows of the Citibank building lie the ruins of Panamá Viejo and its ancient fortress. The native Kuna Yala tribes sell their traditional *molas* on colonial Spanish embankments in Casco Viejo. The sacred and the profane really do exist side by side here. There are parts of the city where casinos, whorehouses (officially called massage parlors) and Catholic churches essentially occupy space on the same block. The grave disparity of wealth and the annexation of nature to economic progress only serve to make these contradictions even more vivid and palpable. On the surface, it would seem that Panamá would make an ideal proving ground for some intense theatre.

    Panamá's contradictions, however, exist within a framework of tradition. The powerful and wealthy are bred from a small circle of elite families, the cycle of poverty and discrimination among Panamá's poor repeats with each new generation, and, of course, the presence and influence of the Roman Catholic Church is felt in all aspects of Panamanian life. It was no surprise to find that the traditional musical reigns supreme in Panamá. They are everywhere and very well attended. In a country where the average secretary makes maybe $400 a month, if you are going to spend your money on theatre you probably want to "forget your troubles, come on get happy!". Who wouldn't?

Protests are common here. One protest, in particular, I can recall quite vividly. I had just passed a theatre where a very popular sold-out production of *Nunsense* was playing. Suddenly, I heard a gunshot, turned to my left, and realized that I was only 50 or so feet away from the police who were trying to subdue students firing projectiles from a homemade cannon. Soon after the gunshot, I was overtaken by remnants of pepper spray emanating from the discarded shells. I had accidently walked into the middle of a riot. Somehow I missed the police in gas masks, the people holding handkerchiefs to their face, and the lack of traffic on the street. This is what I get for trying to solve a complicated production problem over my cell phone and losing sight of what was happening in the real world. Story of my life.

After walking a safe distance across the street, washing off my face and waiting for the burning sensation in my throat to subside, I noticed that the people watching this event play out seemed almost numb to it all. "This happens all the time," said one bystander. "It is normal." For me this was far from normal – it was extraordinary, absurd. We had just finished *JAAF* and were getting ready to produce a line-up of work by U.S. Latina/o playwrights for the upcoming Educational Latin American Theatre Exchange (ELATE) festival at the National Theatre of Panamá that, in addition to Elaine, included the other Elaine (Romero), Jorge Ignacio Cortiñas, Marisela Treviño Orta, and the incomparable María Irene Fornes. The subject matter ranged from gay coming of age to femicide. Bravery was taking on a whole new meaning.

Six months earlier I began to search for plays to produce that would challenge the status quo – both in theatrical form and by questioning accepted social mores. Plays that could bring a new awareness of theatrical possibility were sought. Of course if they could do this through humor, even better. Panamanians love to laugh – at times it appears to be their greatest self-defense mechanism. Elaine's plays fit the bill.

When I first read *JAAF* and *Quality: The Shoe Play*, the titles intrigued me – good start. As a director one of my greatest strengths is my theatrical ADHD – I get bored easily – so if you can get a reaction out of me with the title, yeah, I'm gonna turn the page. Superficial of me, perhaps, but great plays with boring titles end up on in the "thanks, but not thanks" pile all the time. Actually, I hoped the unexpected nature of the titles would serve as a sneak preview of what was to come. I was not disappointed. With my low boredom tolerance, something must be consistently happening to hold my interest. The human behavior being explored, the conflict taking place, must regularly surprise and intrigue me or I'm off looking at the bad masking in the theatre or becoming way too aware of how much my ass is hurting from sitting in an uncomfortable seat. I was immediately and consistently engaged throughout and, more importantly, after having read these plays. I was in Panamá and these were plays right here and right now I needed to work on. Call it an emotional connection, call it good writing. Whatever it was, my reaction to Elaine's plays was in every sense of the word - immediate. I wasn't the only one.

So … what is "immediate" for me? Let's see…well…I was compelled and convicted– read "felt something strongly" – by the questions her characters seemed to be exploring. Why can't I express my passions freely? Where is the beauty in difference? What is the price of quality? Why should I be ashamed of my orgasms? Why do I create? Does breaking *their* rules equal death? These questions seem to spring from the dark side of humanity. One of the beauties of Elaine's writing, however, is that she can take the voiceless and make their plights resonate through humor. Though there certainly is a lot of laughter to be mined in Elaine's plays, she does not swerve from or ease the pain of stark reality either. She is unflinching that way. She does not force hope upon us, but leaves us questioning the nature of hope itself. These plays leave the audience asking themselves, "What next?" What we do with the experience – the hope we create, if any - is up to us. I felt empowered by this.

JAAF and *Quality* are "quick" plays. The characters never "talk" about anything – they are too busy doing. They don't think; they act. Their needs are too strong to linger long in one place. If they stopped to think, all is lost. The action is streamlined, the characters precise, there is no fluff – who has time for that anyway? Audiences were busy laughing or recovering from a swift blow to the stomach during these productions. This is how I like my theatre.

When Pippa suddenly channels the spirit of an ancient Roman woman through a gladiator shoe in a last ditch effort to get Roxanne to hire her, she does so in a sense of what feels to be life and death urgency – she must succeed in this moment, there is no other choice. Nearly one third of Panamanians live in poverty. Some in shacks literally in the shadows of the skyscraper headquarters of multinational corporations. This struggle to satisfy basic needs, to rise above extreme conditions can be felt in Pippa's fight to get the job at *Tremendulos*. The vulnerability of this moment, the tears this actress sheds as she expresses her gratitude touches audiences deeply here. The grace shown by Roxanne in giving her the job is experienced as a miracle, an act of salvation – a literal life and death moment. This play was resonating in ways we could not have imagined.

Elaine's trust in her path, her characters, the production team is... well...maybe a key ingredient in what made these productions so dynamic and energized. In *JAAF*, the freedom to order the scenes as needed or "as determined by the production" is a testament to this trust. The 35 scenes or so were performed in a little less than 50 minutes. This kept the audiences guessing and sometimes the cast. The production was done as if a caravan of actors just dropped into this room and decided to perform this little play. Audiences seemed to be uncomfortable in a good way. That kind of uncomfortable that comes from sitting on the edge of your seat. That kind of uncomfortable that makes you laugh when you catch a glimpse of yourself in the mirror and are forced to look at "how things may really be." That kind of uncomfortable that accompanies experiencing too many "private" feelings in a "public" space. It is an understatement to say that *JAAF* generated much discussion among theatre artists and audiences alike. It was humid and sticky in Panamá – this space did not have air conditioning - and this play was hot. The cast and audience were soaked by the end of their 50-minute workout, but that did not stop the discussion. "I am not done with this play yet," says one local theatre director. The bar downstairs profited from the heat that was being generated.

"It is pretty common for a boy to lose his virginity to a prostitute here," reveals a young actress. "No one talks about it, but it happens." Of course I had to pry – I'm rude that way – I wanted to know more. Apparently this rite of passage involves a father, uncle, and or other close male relative escorting the young man to a brothel. Prostitution is legal in Panamá. Many of the girls are originally from neighboring Columbia and prostitutes can be found throughout the city, in hotels, certain bars, "massage parlors", casinos, and strip clubs. They are tested (supposedly) for STDs once a week. This serves as a selling point I suppose. "My friend did not want to go, but they made him go," reveals the young actress. She acknowledged that at least partial motivation behind this practice was to make sure the young man did not turn out to be a *maricon* – a fag. The confessions seemed to be pouring forth now – something seemed to come unleashed in her. "It was kind of like rape," she declares in a manner that suggested equal amounts of discovery and disgust. "How sad is that? ...That's why this play is important. People need to talk about these things so they can stop them from happening." Elaine was present for this conversation and I cannot do adequate justice in writing as to what this revelation must have meant to her on so many levels. From her expression, I suspect she knew how lucky she was as a playwright to have experienced this moment first hand.

"Elaine's writing pushes buttons." Not one of my more profound insights as a director or teacher, but, nevertheless, this was my response to some general question from a student concerning my interest in the plays. A quick side conversation broke out between other students, culminating in a moment of unmistaken titillation. "Let's do the play in a push-button," suggests a grad student. "What?" The joke eludes me. Attitudes toward sex seem to be little dark secrets rarely talked about, and when they are discussed they are usually framed as naughty jokes. In that respect, Panamá reminded me a little bit of the Midwest. I didn't let it go. "What is so funny?" Needless to say, the rest of the class became a "sex education – Panamá style" course. Apparently "push-buttons" are a type of hotel where room keys suddenly appear and doors magically open with the swipe of a credit card. They are the clandestine playgrounds of extramarital affairs. Everything that happens and everyone who enters ultimately only exist as numbers on a financial statement. I'd be lying if I didn't entertain, just for a brief second, the grad student's suggestion – I'm naughty that way. *Jane Austen* in a "push-button" in Panamá? Can you imagine? It would have been David Rabe's *Hurlyburly* meets Caryl Churchill's *Cloud Nine*. Ah, well…the moment has passed. I suppose some borders are only meant to be questioned, not crossed. For now.

In both *JAAF* and *Quality*…, we are in the presence of heroic women. They occupy that precarious space between social convention and justice. And the price of occupying that space is personal sacrifice. Whether it is Jane sacrificing her social position, the Writer sacrificing precious moments with her child, or Roxanne sacrificing her dignity, they all readily do so, in spite of the pain, to follow a deeply personal truth. And they do not compromise. Why should they have to? These women's struggles are epic, timeless, and never-ending. They are paving a way – a new way – to travel. Where it leads …

In many ways their heroism is rooted in their work. Elaine's heroines use their work as a means to discover and carve out new paths. They all work very hard and this seems to give them the strength to deal with life. There's no doubt that daily struggle is the way of life for the characters in these plays. These characters could easily be overwhelmed by their circumstances, but instead of caving to pressures they seem to be energized by the struggle. Self-pity is not in their vocabulary.

Jane's desire to liberate herself from suffocating definitions placed on her by society resonates strongly with the cast and audiences. Her hungry scream for freedom seems to spring from a deeper core in this place where the concept of "freedom" is, at best, intangible and conditional. For Elaine's characters the words they write, speak, dream, scream are their source of liberation –

refuge and weapon. They love with them – they kill with them. They know how to use them – they are smart. You may resist them, but you can't dismiss them. Upon a return visit, one man remarked, "I hated this play, but I was compelled to see it again." Something was being awakened with this production. In a little upper room theatre in the Casco Viejo district of Panamá City, in an intimate, yet profound way, a kind of history was being made. "…maybe it was something in me I hated," the same man later suggested.

    Men rule Panamá. Machismo reigns supreme with many men maintaining superiority and dominance over the women in their family, often restricting their freedom inside and outside the home. This behavior is exacerbated by unemployment, poverty, and often heightened by alcohol. Inflexible social attitudes bring about women's dependence on men and forces them into difficult situations they would otherwise avoid. Alarming rates of domestic violence, especially femicide, exist here.

    Not all men exhibit these qualities. Not all women tolerate this behavior. Certainly there are strong women in Panamá who are breaking down the oppression and degradation embodied in the likes of the push-button. Panamá has even had a woman president. Like I said, Panamá is a land of contradictions rooted in tradition. Elaine's plays were written for places like this. I have been around the block now once or twice and it is fair to say that Elaine's plays tell people things that they won't hear elsewhere – shows them things they won't see elsewhere. The writing feels vital. It is clear from working with Elaine that she is a writer who deeply feels that *something* that needs to be said. Yes, indeed, these plays were going to push buttons here. But instead of creating a hiding place for human behavior, they were going to thrust it into the light.

The success of the productions can be contributed in large part to this spirit of collaboration beyond borders. From the beginning, this process was as much an in-depth intercultural educational experience as anything. Everyone involved with the projects seemed to have used the opportunity to celebrate and explore differences as opposed to dwelling on the difficulties these difficulties presented. During *!Zapatos!* (*Quality*), we were blessed to have a fantastic production team, including translator Myrna Castro, and the actresses Mariela Aragon Chiari and Maritza Vernaza. During the early rehearsals the actresses seemed to connect deeply to the politics of these two women. At times it felt like we were playing in a minefield while exploring how power struggles between women manifest themselves -especially in a country where women's rights exist perhaps more in theory than actual practice. Behaviors and feelings held back for what must have been years by these women seemed to be liberated in these rehearsals. We were exploring common ground and untraversed terrain at the same time. We were drawing new connections between the commerce of art and *ecoturismo* - the selling of Panamá's environment for the sake of tourism dollars. The intercultural nature of the project was allowing the play to expand its reach in ways that could not have been predicted.

I suffer, as does Elaine, from that particular condition of certain theatre artists blessed to reside in that space between reality and illusion, fated to stand in the gap and shine our own peculiar light on the connections between the two. It is October now in Park Hills, Missouri as I am finishing up this introduction. I am visiting my parents who are celebrating their 47th wedding anniversary and I am reminded of the older married couple from the scene "a la tiempo" in *JAAF* who reminisce about a beautiful shared moment from their past. In our production, the actors switched parts and performed the scene again. And I wonder what would have happened if it had been possible for my parents to do the same with their marriage. Oh the implications of such thoughts – the implications of such theatre. It really is, ultimately, all about "love" isn't it – simple, but true.

In a few hours I will, as I have done on several occasions now, sign onto SKYPE and check in with the actresses that are now in their *segundo temporado* (2nd run) of *¡Zapatos!* Watching the production with a combination of high definition video cameras via the Internet is a surreal experience. Once again I am reminded of the limitless possibilities of theatre. Maybe this production will pave the way for future collaborations across borders, expanding and redefining accepted norms of "who are you writing for?" Will it take bravery on the part of artists and producers? Sure. Will it take innovation? Most definitely. Is it unavoidable? Yep. As technology continues to advance at breakneck speeds and we attempt to make sense of the great social phenomenon of our time – globalization – the need for intercultural theatre collaboration will become even more self-evident. Is it worth it? Depends upon your definition of "worth". Based upon the experiences of the past year – I can't wait to do it again!

"I can do this. I am going to do this!" declares a woman graduate student who has always wanted to write plays. Elaine wanted to teach a playwriting workshop to the students – she is gracious that way. Her presence was empowering in more ways than one. As theatre artists, most of us hope that our work will make a difference – whatever the hell that means. Our little fleeting productions are gone as quickly as they appear in the relative scope of one's life journey in the theatre. Whether measurable or intangible, perhaps it is some lasting impact – inspiration for future change-makers –

the beginnings of someone finding their voice – that, if we are lucky, our work purposes. To quote Elaine, "The future of the theatre belongs to those who have not yet spoken." Of all the accolades the productions received – and there were many – this single, solitary declaration of the graduate student mingled with "…maybe it was something in me I hated" and the whispered, "This is brave writing", that serve as the ultimate testament of this experience and the potential inherent in Elaine Avila writing.

Ted Gregory

October, 2011

JANE AUSTEN, ACTION FIGURE

by Elaine Avila

Voted "Best Production/Audience Favorite"
by audiences at the 2011
International Festival de Cocos, **Panamá City, Panamá**

PREMIERES (*Ensemble members played a variety of roles*)
StageLab Festival, Edmonton, AB, Canada, June 2011
Director: Kathleen Weiss
Jane Austen....Melissa Thingelstad
Daughter.....Molly Flood
Doctor....Clinton Carew
Mr. Darcy.....Thrasso Petras

Teatro Lagartija, Panamá City, Panamá, February 2011
In Spanish, as *Jane Austen, la Figura de Acción*
Translated by Myrna Castro, Director: Ted Gregory
Jane Austen/Emily Dickinson.....Myrna Castro
Doctor....Alex Mariscal
Agatha......Masha Armuelles Voinova
Aphra Behn.....Clara Tristan
Lover.....Ramon Cardenes

WORKSHOP HISTORY
New York City, New York, Fall 2008, Director: Heidi Carlsen; Tricklock Theatre Company, Albuquerque, New Mexico, Fall 2009, Director: Kathleen Weiss; Women's Project, New York City, Winter 2010, Director: Heidi Carlsen; *Jane Austen, Action Figure...and other short plays* was developed and workshopped at the PTC Colony on November 2010. Playwrights Theatre Centre, Vancouver, BC, Canada Fall 2010, Dramaturge: D.D. Kugler; *Jane Austen, la Figura de Acción* was workshopped at the Universidad de

Panamá in November/December 2010 with the following cast:
Jane Austen: Maritza Vernaza, Writer: Mariela Aragón Chiari, Ensemble: Masha Armuelles Voinova, Alex Mariscal, Ileana Solis, Natir Argüello, Carlos Bermudez, Irene Bermudez, Ramon Cardenes, Jaime Noel Canto, Meredith Carley, Daniel Gomez Nates, Efrain Gonzólez, Marisin Hernández, Argelia Lashington, María Eleiza Oses, Orlando Osovio, Maximino Quirós Sánchez, Lissette Rodriguez, María Antonia Taylor, Lesdy Torres, and Clara Tristan

PERFORMANCE HISTORY
Premiere, "19th Century O" Working Theatre Collective, Portland Oregon, Feb. 2010 Director: Ashley Hollingshead

SPECIAL THANKS: Caridad Svich, Mac Wellman, Suzan-Lori Parks, Erik Ehn, D.D. Kugler, Kathleen Weiss, Heidi Taylor, Martin Kinch, Elyne Quan, Brian Fidler, Andrew Templeton, Ron Lea, Andrew McNee, Karin Konoval, Nicola Lipman, Luisa Jojic, Heidi Carlsen, Donna Jewell, Bill Clark, Juli Hendren, Cristina Anselmo, Susy May, Elizabeth Palmer, Elizabeth Johnson, Ian Johnson, Jessica di' Giovanni, Samara Naeymi, Leonard Madrid, Amanda Duarte, Bobby Placensia, Kate Schroeder, Clara Tristan, the Tristan Family, Ted Gregory, Myrna Castro, Karin Coonrod

Thrasso Petras as Mr. Darcy and Melissa Thingelstad as Jane Austen, in Stage Lab Production of Jane Austen, Action Figure, June 2011, directed by Kathleen Weiss (photo: Josiah Hiemstra, courtesy of Stage Lab Festival, Canadian Centre for Theatre Creation and the University of Alberta)

CHARACTERS:

There are 43 characters. They can be played by 2 women and 2 men. It is suggested that recurring characters be played by the same actor(s). There is a version for 3 women and 2 men, please request this from the author, if needed.

Jane Austen
Voice Over Voice/Mr. Darcy/Mrs. Bennett (Elizabeth's Mother)/Death
Jane's Brother
Cassandra (Jane's sister)
Caroline (Jane's Niece)
Edward (Jane's Nephew)
Miss Bingley
Elizabeth Bennett
Doctor
Agatha
Fiancé
Woman
Man
Woman
A
B
Guide
Tourist
Woman
Mother
Man
Woman
Mama
Girl
Famous Author
Groupie One
Groupie Two

Groupie Three
Tigre
Josefina, Tigre's fling, a Wife/Mother/Daughter
Maria, Josefina's Mother
João
Hilda
Hope
Promise
Aphra Behn
Lover
Emily Dickinson
Susie
Man

JANE AUSTEN, ACTION FIGURE
For Donna Jewell

    (Jane at a small, small writing desk, writing.)

VOICE OVER VOICE: She sits, she writes, she turns heartbreak into literature.

JANE: Mr. Darcy! *(she laughs to herself)*

JANE'S BROTHER: *(entering)* Ja----ne.

    (Sound of a storm of children.)

VOICE OVER VOICE: Under the blotter. Jane hides...her masterpiece.

    (Jane quickly hides her writing under the blotter on the small, small desk.)

VOICE OVER VOICE: Jane uses her powers of concentration to...hold. Her. Thought.

JANE: O! Brother!

JANE'S BROTHER: I find I cannot string my thoughts together with the children about. Watch them would you?

JANE: O, dear. Watch the children. Is their mother ill?

JANE'S BROTHER: Indisposed.

VOICE OVER VOICE: Not to be thwarted, Jane uses her deductive reasoning superpowers.

JANE: My dearest sister-in-law, indisposed, again? There was much drinking of sherry, night the last.

JANE'S BROTHER: Oh, the trials I must endure.

JANE: How terrible for you.

JANE'S BROTHER: Fortunately you are so good with the children.

JANE: I am? Oh, yes, I am.

VOICE OVER VOICE: Jane uses her politeness super powers to bite. Her. Tongue.

JANE'S BROTHER: I'll fetch them for you.

JANE: Thank you brother.

> *(Brother exits. Sound of a storm of children. Jane quickly makes a note on her writing.)*

JANE'S BROTHER: I'm off-- to stride the moors and the heath.

JANE: Sounds divine.

VOICE OVER VOICE: The storm of children bursts upon the stage. Jane, only a nanosecond to spare—WRITES! She is Jane Austen, Action Figure.

JANE: *(smiles, looks at audience)* Thank you.

19th CENTURY "O"

DOCTOR: *(speaking into Dictaphone)* Patient A. Listless, disturbed, distressed. I connect her pelvis to the vibrating machine. She convulses, becomes flushed, and then the color returns to her cheeks. It is my dream to thus revive all the listless women of England.

AGATHA: *(stirring, on the table behind him)* Doctor, I feel so refreshed after your treatment. Can I come back tomorrow? Can I come back in an hour? In fifteen minutes? In five? Can I come back now?

(Doctor backs away from Agatha, fearfully)

DOCTOR: I cannot treat you continually. What of my dream? To revive all the women of England? Agatha. Patient A. Restrain yourself. Please. I am a charitable, reasonable—

AGATHA: Doctor, don't you like restoring color to my cheeks…

DOCTOR: I do.

AGATHA: The rhythm of the machine.

DOCTOR: I do.

AGATHA: My convulsing pelvis.

DOCTOR: You have become lewd.

AGATHA: You have become stingy with your power over me.

DOCTOR: Too bad. *(he exits)*

AGATHA: Soon I discovered I could attach my fiancé to my pelvis and achieve the same results, whether by hand, mouth, elbow, toe, armpit, or other unmentionable areas.

FIANCE: Agatha, you suck.

AGATHA: He too, turned on me.

FIANCE: You suck me in, you suck like a seccubus.

AGATHA: Succubi suck. A verity. You are so good with words.

FIANCE: Let me speak plain. I wish you to be more like other fiancés. I am grateful when you relieve me when I need it, yes, thank you, but, I tire of our "hobby." Why don't you go print up some little calling cards and go leave them on a little silver trays at neighbors' homes?

AGATHA: Why?

FIANCE: This is what women do. Call on others. They find the others otherwise occupied and must then leave little cards on little silver trays.

AGATHA: Sounds dreadful. What if we used our noses? Our pinky fingers? Our earlobes? I've never gotten relief from an earlobe before. Have you?

FIANCE: You are becoming wanton. Unmanageable. Unmarriageable!

AGATHA: But we did the same thing.

FIANCE: Always with the weak willed reasoning of a woman.

AGATHA: I am a woman.

FIANCE: Not any more. You are a whore.

AGATHA: You made me one. *(he exits)* I fell into a pit of despair. I considered returning to the doctor and asking to have my female organs removed. They seemed to cause me no end of difficulty. Fortunately, I did not. I discovered I am an inventor, an entrepreneur. I decided to open my own little shop. I hung various false signs, Haberdashery. Suffragettes. Temperance. *(A woman enters)* Women glutted the little medieval lane outside my door. *(The woman hands Agatha a large wad of old British bank notes.)* I turned a simply marvelous profit. *(Agatha wheels out a massive machine with tubes and pumps. Wraps it in a blanket, gives it to the woman.)* I sold those splendid machines. You know. The ones that doctor introduced to my pelvis, so many moons ago.

WOMAN: Thank you, Agatha. Thank for the…

AGATHA: Let's call it temperance, shall we? Remember, darling, pretend and be prudent.

WOMAN: Aye. Pretend and be prudent.

(Agatha kisses her on both cheeks and sends her on her way.)

AGATHA: Toodleloo.

LONELY 1

(Woman staring into space. Noise of a party. She is the loneliest person in the world. Man enters.)

MAN: You look like the loneliest person in the world.

WOMAN: I'm not.

MAN: I hate these things, don't you?

WOMAN: They have their purpose.

MAN: Let's take off. Into the night. See the stars, feel the wild hot breeze on our skin...

WOMAN: I can't.

MAN: Why not?

WOMAN: Isn't done.

MAN: They've taught us all this stuff. Be safe. Be prudent.

WOMAN: Kiss me.

(Man kisses woman passionately.)

MAN: See? I would never hurt you.

WOMAN: Never.

MAN: Why would I? Your insides, your outs, they're beautiful.

WOMAN: Let's experience. It all. Nature, freedom, youth, pleasure.

MAN: Okay.

(They run off together.)

PACKING
For JHA

(A is packing, bringing more and more objects on stage and putting them into a large suitcase. B enters.)

B: We don't need all that.

A: We do.

B: *(holds up jar of jam)* ?

A: It's really good.

B: They'll have it there.

A: What if they don't?

B: *(holds up sheet)?*

A: 10,000 count. So soft.

B: *(picking up suitcase)* So heavy.

A: When Queen Elizabeth travels, she packs everything, sheets, jam, everything.

B: When she goes to the White House, she won't sleep on their sheets?

A: She won't.

B: When she travels to Canada, she won't eat our[1] jam?

A: Correct.

B: Canadian jam is terrific.

A: She'll never know.

B: What about letting life unfold?

A: Hmm.

B: Nothing to carry, nothing to declare.

A: Nothing.

B: Fine by me.

A: No…toothpaste.

B: No.

A: Would you buy some there?

B: Maybe.

A: Imagine, days and nights with no toothpaste.

B: Fun.

---

[1] When performed in America, please say "their" jam

A: Spending your limited time in a foreign land, shopping for toothpaste.

B: I like the people I get to meet.

A: What sort of people?

B: Tooth paste purveyors. Apothocaries. Watching the people of the country possibly brush their teeth with alternative methods, handed down through the centuries.

A: What methods? Like brushing your teeth with…twigs?

(B nods and smiles, A shudders.)

SILENCE
for Kate Schroeder and Jessica di'Giovanni

MOTHER: No daughter of mine—I never want to see no daughter of mine walking downtown without a purpose.

WOMAN: I was looking in windows.

MOTHER: You were walking aimlessly. Laughing. Gallivanting. It looks bad.

WOMAN: I was with a friend.

MOTHER: Gallivanting.

WOMAN: A female friend.

MOTHER: You're married now. Your husband can't get ahead in business if his wife looks like a—like a--walking without a purpose, with no particular aim, no aim. You'll never do it again.

WOMAN: No. Of course not.

PLAY TODAY

*(Mama is leaving for work by bike.
Little girl runs out onto a porch.)*

GIRL: Mama, mama! What's your play about today?

MAMA: Princesses. Snakes. Crocodiles. Cockroaches. Women Astronauts. What's your play about?

GIRL: Uh—I don't know. Horses! Horses! Mama, mama! What's your play about today?

MAMA: Leaving for work. The passage of time. Growing old. What's yours about?

GIRL: Barbie. Spongebob. Toy story. What's your play about?

MAMA: Propaganda inducing children to buy toys.

BREATHLESS

GUIDE: Today, forbidden cities of the world.

TOURIST: I'm--

GUIDE: Tomorrow, the Taj Majal, the Great Wall of China, Machu Picchu. Meet at the bus at 3 a.m.

TOURIST: I'm tired.

GUIDE: Ungrateful.

TOURIST: I'm grateful.

GUIDE: At 3 a.m. we'll admire the Milky Way galaxy from the Himalayas—hopefully it won't be too cloudy. Ah! To see the arms of the Milky Way, filled with stars, spiraling out from our lovely planet.

TOURIST: I need down time.

GUIDE: Why?

TOURIST: I need one day with no agendas.

GUIDE: Your holiday is short. I can show you everything.

TOURIST: I can't enjoy it if I'm tired.

GUIDE: You can rest when your holiday is over.

TOURIST: I want to rest now.

GUIDE: You can rest when you're dead.

TOURIST: I need to stare into space. Inner space. Wander. Wonder. Sort. Stretch. Sitting in one spot. A bench. Knowing every nick and cut, curve and chip. Who walks by. And how. This tree. How leaves fall—sometimes all at once. Sometimes, slowly, over weeks. Then the branches, barren, exquisite against the sky.

GUIDE: But I—

TOURIST: I know. It's okay.

GUIDE: Show you—

TOURIST: Sit with me.

GUIDE: *(pause)* I can't. *(antsy, running off)* Pick you up at 6 a.m. tomorrow?

TOURIST: Fine. Yes.

A WALK (1)

> *Adapted from Jane Austen's* <u>Pride and Prejudice</u>
> *(Sound of a storm of children, leaving. Jane collapses over her small, small writing desk)*

VOICE OVER VOICE: Having provided for her brother's solace and cared for the children, Jane Austen writes her masterpiece---

JANE: *(weakly)* I wish my brother would watch his own children…that I might string. My thoughts… while striding… the heath. Ah…so does my character, Elizabeth Bennett…

ELIZABETH: Walking is my only alternative.

VOICE OVER VOICE: She is Jane Austen, Action--

JANE: *(to Voice Over Voice)* Would you be a dear? And play Elizabeth Bennett's mum?

VOICE OVER VOICE: Of course!

ELIZABETH: Walking is my only alternative.

MOTHER *(played by VOICE OVER VOICE)*: Elizabeth, how can you be so silly, as to think of such a thing in all this dirt!

JANE: Dirt! *(giggles)*

ELIZABETH: Mama, the distance is nothing, only three miles.

(Miss Bingley enters)

MOTHER *(played by VOICE OVER VOICE)*: Oh, Elizabeth, it's Miss Bingley.

MISS BINGLEY: Why must *she* be scampering about the country? Her hair so untidy--So blowsy!

JANE: Blowsy.

MOTHER *(Played by VOICE OVER VOICE)*: She really looked almost wild. Yes, and her petticoat; I hope you saw her petticoat, six inches deep in mud!

JANE: Mud.

MISS BINGLEY: It shows an abominable sort of conceited independence.

JANE: Abominable. *(giggles)*

A WALK (3)

MAN: A woman was tacked to a tree and raped repeatedly over there. Didja know that?

WOMAN: Uh, why, no, I did not know that.

MAN: You still gonna walk there?

WOMAN: It's on the way to the market. I need food.

MAN: Sheesh. Another woman was cornered by six men, you gotta watch out for the local men, and beaten to death. After she was raped. Repeatedly.

WOMAN: Hmm.

MAN: I wouldn't want to be a woman alone. Around here.

WOMAN: You live alone.

MAN: Ya, sure, ha! But I'm not a woman.

WOMAN: You walk to the market.

MAN: Ya, I'm not worried.

WOMAN: We're not that different.

MAN: Ya, but it ain't gonna happen to me. Thems the breaks. You prepared?

WOMAN: For what?

MAN: You got some weapons over there?

WOMAN: What kind of weapons?

MAN: Guns, mace, sirens. Bear spray.

WOMAN: No.

MAN: Jeez. You serious? You're going for a walk around this town, where you don't speak the language, and the locals, they're gonna do god knows what to you and you don't have a weapon? You're totally unprepared.

WOMAN: ----

(He exits. She walks, terrified, but brave.)

PLAY TODAY 2

GIRL: Can I have a Woody Doll? Like in "Toy Story"? Can I have a Wedding Barbie? I want Wedding Barbie!

MAMA: We don't have TV! Not even Basic Cable! Where do you get these…desires?

GIRL: Please! My friend has Wedding Barbie!

MAMA: I played with Barbie.

GIRL: Please—

MAMA: Big bags of Barbies from big sisters we'd dump onto the lawn and make our own village—

GIRL: Please--

MAMA: Would you like to play village?

GIRL: Sure!

MAMA: Once upon a time, we lived in villages. People would make toys out of anything—

GIRL: Like what?

MAMA: Uh. Twigs.

GIRL: Twigs? That's funny!

MAMA: And there were all sorts of types of people—

GIRL: Wedding Barbie?

MAMA: There is always a Wedding Barbie—

GIRL: Even in the olden times?

MAMA: Brides have been big for a long, long time.

GIRL: Was there Spongebob?

MAMA: No—*(sees girl's distress)* But there were sponges. And bobs. Oh--gotta go. What's your play about today?

GIRL: Barbie. Spongebob. Toy story. What's your play about?

MAMA: The appropriation of our imaginations by multinational corporations.

LONELY 2

A: I'm lonely.

B: Shut up.

A: That's cruel.

B: It's cruel to say you're lonely.

A: Why? I am lonely.

B: Hello. I'm right here.

A: Why don't you talk to me?

B: I am talking to you.

A: I mean about something, anything substantive.

B: Oo. Big word. Substantive. It sounds like oatmeal.

A: Substantive. We are talking about you and me. How we get along. If that isn't substantive, I don't know what is.

B: Substantive. Things that have substance. Meaning.

A: I know what it means.

B: Go to bed.

A: Please.

B: I'm turning out the light.

A: Please.

HEARTBREAK

(Jane and Cassandra, each looking in a mirror, weeping, heartbroken.)

JANE: O, sister.

CASSANDRA: Dear Jane. We look a wreck. Mother expects to see all our wanton tendrils in place.

JANE: I concede that I may have been unsatisfactory in my courtship, but surely she cannot fault you Cassandra for not being married. Your fiancé died!

(Cassandra begins weeping.)

VOICE OVER VOICE: Only literary accomplishment can save you Jane.

JANE: *(screams)*.

CASSANDRA: What ever is wrong with you Jane? Think of our sisters. They still have a chance to make a match. We have to get ready for the ball.

JANE : Yes, I know.

VOICE OVER VOICE: She sits, she writes, she turns heartbreak into literature.

JANE: NO. I do NOT.

CASSANDRA: You do not what? *(Jane shakes her head)*

JANE: *(to Voice over Voice)* I'm occupied with getting my wanton tendrils in place so my sisters can get married!

VOICE OVER VOICE: Literary accomplish—

JANE: NO!
(Voice over voice collapses, dejected, over the small, small writing desk.)

CASSANDRA: Um. Have you heard from him?

JANE: Who?

CASSANDRA: Tom! What precisely transpired between you two?

JANE: "Imagine everything most profligate and shocking in the way of dancing and sitting down together."[2]

CASSANDRA: O. Lord. I cannot.

JANE: You can. What else have we to do?

CASSANDRA: It does sound…delicious.

JANE: Tom might have forgotten me—

CASSANDRA: He has not.

JANE: He was told to. I am not of the right class. Marriage is a bargain of class. But I have not forgotten him. *(she pulls a picture from her dress)* Look at the soft curl of his lip. Imagine kissing such a churlish lip…

CASSANDRA: Jane!

JANE: Imagine feeding such a lip the most exotic fruits and vegetables…

CASSANDRA: Jane!

JANE: And feeding him parts of one's own body. Imagine feasting on him.

---

[2] Tomalin, C. (1997) *Jane Austen – A Life*. Viking.

CASSANDRA: Where do you get these thoughts?

JANE: From him. This is his favorite book. *(She pulls a copy of* Tom Jones *from her dress. Cassandra begins reading, greedily, and giggling)*

CASSANDRA: O. My.

JANE: See what solace a book might provide in our time of need?

CASSANDRA: Aye. O. My.

VOICE OVER VOICE: Sounds like a...literary accomplishment...Ja—ane...you too can provide solace—

JANE: Za— truly?

VOICE OVER VOICE: In times of need.

JANE: The History of Tom Jones—A Foundling is a great book. Fielding is a great writer.

VOICE OVER VOICE: How do you know you aren't?

JANE: Aren't what?

VOICE OVER VOICE: A great writer.

JANE: Fielding is a man.

VOICE OVER VOICE: How much more might YOUR words make Cassandra laugh?

JANE: I do not presume—

VOICE OVER VOICE: Please Jane. Presume.

CASSANDRA: Who are you are you speaking to?

JANE: Uh—my characters.

CASSANDRA: Splendid. Let's forget our tendrils and be merry 'til Mother returns. It's been so long since I've felt joy.

VOICE OVER VOICE: *(whispers, pulls out a chair for Jane, puts a quill in her hand)* Sit. Write. Turn heartbreak into literature.

JANE: *(writes)* "Mr. Darcy was not all he seemed to be…"

VOICE OVER VOICE: Her faith renewed in the power of the written word, Jane continues her masterpiece. She is Jane Austen, Action Figure.

(Cassandra continues reading, gasping, giggling.)

JANE: Thank you.

HOTEL TERRA NOSTRA
for Bill Clark Sr.

(Daughter is running and climbing and jumping, hanging off of Mama. Mama is trying to write, on a small, small writing desk.)

VOICE OVER VOICE: She sits. She writes. She turns heartbreak into literature.

MAMA: Are you talking to me?

VOICE OVER VOICE: She sits—

MAMA: *(sits)* Okay.

VOICE OVER VOICE: She writes.

MAMA: *(writes)* "When Agnes—"

GIRL: Mama, mama, mama. *(Mama continues writing)* Apple juice? Please? Please?

MAMA: Yes, yes, apple juice--*(she stops, rummages in bag, finds apple juice box, hands it to daughter).*

VOICE OVER VOICE: Not to be thwarted, she—concentrates—

MAMA: *(writing)* "Nestled in..."

GIRL: *(slurps apple juice dry, hands box to mama.)*

MAMA: Apple juice....*(writes)* "The clerk at the Hotel Terra Nostra was hiding..."

GIRL: A quesadilla.

MAMA: I'll get it for you in just a... "The clerk was hiding her writing under the--"

GIRL: I have to go potty.

MAMA: Under the potty—under a blotter...yes, surrealism, yes, honey—which is it? Potty? Quesadilla? Potty.

VOICE OVER VOICE: *(begins to leave)*

MAMA: No! Don't go! I need super-powers—

VOICE OVER VOICE: *(smiles, shakes his head, exits)*

GIRL: I'm hungry. I don't have to go potty.

MAMA: *(collapses, digs in handbag, hands her a quesadilla, sighs)*

GIRL: Mama—why don't you write about being a mama?

MAMA: Good idea. Can't take a walk— *(writes on sleeve)*

GIRL: Why are you writing on your sleeve?

MAMA: To remember. I'm your chair—

GIRL: That's funny.

MAMA: Your bed, your restaurant, your bathroom porter, your vomitorium— your whirligig. I'm your whirligig! *(picks her up and whirls her around, spinning, laughing with her daughter.)*

GIRL: Mama, mama, mama, mama...

MAMA: Whirl-ee- gig! You're my whirl-ee-gig.

(They laugh.)

Writing Star I

(A radiant woman author enters the stage. Groupies start to crowd her, them sit, enthralled and in awe.)

FAMOUS AUTHOR: I'm inspired by the beauty of the desert. The dry air frees my mind. But I feel such sorrow that the earth here has been poisoned by the testing of nuclear weapons. The feminine is very, very beautiful. Beautiful and powerful. The feminine will rise, no matter what cruelty is inflicted upon it.

GROUPIE ONE: Famous author, I put affirmations all over my house. If I'm angry, I know it means a child in Burma may be killed. That's why I'm never angry.

FAMOUS AUTHOR: Thich Nhat Hahn, the great Buddhist teacher, says we must take care of our anger, comfort it like a crying baby.

GROUPIE ONE: Famous author, who will you vote for?

GROUPIE TWO: Famous author, how do we end war?

GROUPIE THREE: Famous author, how do we end violence against women?

GROUPIE TWO: Famous author, I only wear two outfits. Consumerism must end. Everyone must wear only two outfits.

FAMOUS AUTHOR: I don't want to wear only two outfits.

GROUPIE THREE: Famous author, do you think we'll survive as a species?

FAMOUS AUTHOR: I'm hopeful. But we aren't changing very fast. Maybe the earth, our mother, will have to wipe us out, in order that she survive. The Hopi say this has happened many times.

GROUPIE ONE: Famous author, thank you. You are radiant.

GROUPIE TWO: You are beautiful.

GROUPIE THREE: Famous author, thank you. You've put me back in touch will all I find essential.

GROUPIE TWO: Famous Author, you are beauty itself.

A WALK (2)

(A woman walking down the street like in Ruth Orkin's photo "American Girl in Rome," 1951, that graces the walls of nearly every other coffee bar in North America. Man enters, catcalls her. She is ashamed but still dares to walk down the street. She still dares to be in Italy. The man begins gyrating around her, displaying his body parts.)

MAN: Do you like this? Do you want this?

(Woman bats him off.)

MAN: WHAT DO YOU WANT?

WOMAN: I don't want anything right now!

MAN: C'mon baby. Don't be such a cock tease!

WOMAN: I am—walking-- down-- the street. *(she bats him off)* THAT'S IT.

MAN: But the way you are dressed! The way you walk. Didn't your mama tell you should stay at home? Didn't your mama tell you should have brought your brother?

WOMAN: Jesus! This is the shit we were writing in 1970. Do I have to have a feminist consciousness raising like every single goddam day? Aren't we over this? Aren't we beyond this?

MAN: *(switching to a new age-y persona)* Of course we are. Tell me your fantasies. Tell me what you want.

WOMAN: ......

MAN: Please.

WOMAN: You go first.

MAN: I can't.

WOMAN: Why not?

MAN: Porn starts downloading in my brain.

WOMAN: What's wrong with that? Tell me.

MAN: It's something they sold to me. Not something I made up.

WOMAN: Who cares? Let's get it on!

MAN: ......

20th Century O
for Amanda Duarte and Bobby Plasencia

(Tigre and Josefina, in bed.)

TIGRE: I've always admired you.

JOSEFINA: Hmmm. Tigre. I love that your name your name means Tiger. Tigre. Tigre. Rrrrr.

(They kiss, remove clothing.)

TIGRE: I have the utmost respect for you.

JOSEFINA: Mmm. Hmmm. Wow. You're in good shape.

TIGRE: I'm on T.V. I have to work out.

JOSEFINA: It must be hard to find the time, what with the long days on set and your angry guests—Tigre. Too bad you lost that big sponsor.

TIGRE: Let's not talk.

(He goes under covers.)

JOSEFINA: Oh! Tigre! Wow!

(Maria enters. Stares at Tigre. Exits.)

TIGRE: Who was that?

JOSEFINA: My mother.

TIGRE: Your mother? What is she doing here?
JOSEFINA: Babysitting.

TIGRE: Who?

JOSEFINA: My kids. I told you I had kids. Weren't you listening?

TIGRE: Why was she staring at me?

JOSEFINA: You're a movie star.

TIGRE: A TV Star.

JOSEFINA: Same difference.

TIGRE: Not to me.

JOSEFINA: Tigre. Tigre. Tigre.

(They kiss.)

TIGRE: It was creepy. The way she stared at me.

JOSEFINA: People stare at you all day long. You're on TV!

TIGRE: Why didn't she stare at you?

JOSEFINA: She thinks this is your fault. Cause I'm married. You know. Latino culture. This would be your fault. I'm weak by nature. You tempted me. You're Latino, right?

TIGRE: I don't think of myself that way.

JOSEFINA: If you respect me so much, why didn't you remember I'm married? That I need babysitting? You don't respect me.

TIGRE: Of course I do.

JOSEFINA: Is this a set up? Is this going to ruin my life? I'm going to be on the Tigre Show, "WOMEN WHO THINK OF THEIR ORGASMS BEFORE THEY THINK OF THEIR FAMILIES." Did someone send you? Why should I trust you? You trick people all day long! Why should I believe you? Why does anyone believe you? This is going to fuck up my marriage!

TIGRE: *No te preocupes.* Don't worry.

(Maria enters, with a shotgun (or a knife). Tigre finds his pants and runs.)

JOSEFINA: I'm sorry Tigre. She likes my husband. You were good in bed. Thanks.

GAME

MAMA: Let's play "Jane Austen, Action Figur—"

GIRL: Okay!

MAMA: *(reading)* "Which man is nasty, which is nice? Win or lose. Life or death." This one is Mr. Darcy— He is a "fine...tall...noble man"[3]

GIRL: He's cute!

MAMA: I know! *(reading)* He has "10,000 a year"[4]. But he is stuck up.

---

[3] From first description of Mr. Darcy; Austen, Jane, *Pride and Prejudice*
[4] Ibid

GIRL: Euww!

MAMA: Mr. Wickham—

GIRL: He's cute!

MAMA: *(Nods)* Right—it says he has 'the best part of beauty—'[5] whew—he sure does! He's a soldier—

GIRL: So he's brave, right?

MAMA: *(she makes a face, shrugs like she can't be sure)* Mr. Bingley—

GIRL: Cute!

MAMA: Mr. Bingley is "gentleman like…pleasant…easy, unaffected manners…"[6] Okay, we're ready to play.

GIRL: Yay!

MAMA: It's your turn.

GIRL: Yay! What do I do? What do I do?

MAMA: You have to figure out… which one is nasty…

GIRL: How do I do that?

MAMA: You… guess…

---

[5] From first description of Mr. Wickham; Austen, Jane, *Pride and Prejudice*

[6] From first description of Mr. Bingley; Austen, Jane, *Pride and Prejudice*

GIRL: Okay, okay, Mr. Bingley?

MAMA: *(makes a face)* No.

GIRL: I lost? I hate this game!

MAMA: Wait, wait—I didn't see this—first, you have to—put on the Jane Austen Secret personality decoder ring!

GIRL: Can I go again?

MAMA: Totally. Okay. Which one is nasty?

GIRL: *(girl makes special secret decoder ring sounds)* Mr…Wickham? WICKHAM!

MAMA: Yes! You won!

GIRL: Yay!

<u>PROPOSAL</u>
for Heidi Carlsen

VOICE OVER VOICE: Jaaane---

JANE: Mmph.

VOICE OVER VOICE: Jaaane---wakest thou—rousest thou—

JANE: Mmmph. Slumber. Mmmph.

VOICE OVER VOICE: You agreed to marry him.

(Jane bolts upright.)

VOICE OVER VOICE: You must admit this bears consideration.

JANE: Marriage!

VOICE OVER VOICE: You accepted his proposal.

JANE: I did.

VOICE OVER VOICE: Marriage will silence me. Will still your pen.

JANE: It need not.

VOICE OVER VOICE: Come Jane, do you believe that?

JANE: No.

VOICE OVER VOICE: We have good times together, do we not? Remember when you wrote…"Splendidly yet unhappily married." [7]

JANE: Did I write that?

VOICE OVER VOICE: "United to a man of double her own age…"[8] You did. You were only sixteen.

JANE: Sixteen?

---

[7] Austen-Leigh, W. / Austen-Leigh, R. (2009) *Jane Austen, Her Life and Letters - A Family Record*. Echo Library.

[8] Ibid

VOICE OVER VOICE: "Whose disposition was not amiable, whose manners were unpleasing…"[9] You must admit you have a certain something Jane.

JANE: But the economic situation of my family—

VOICE OVER VOICE: What do you owe them?

JANE: My very life.

VOICE OVER VOICE: That is what your marriage will take.

JANE: Harris Bigg is the heir to Manydown! I have waited seven years for a proposal such as this—

VOICE OVER VOICE: Za—

JANE: Seven years! Am I to eschew the pleasures of children—

VOICE OVER VOICE: The mania of children—

JANE: The comforts of old age—the delights of the marriage bed…

VOICE OVER VOICE: Risking death in childbirth—

JANE: Ugh… *(collapses, pounds the bed)*

VOICE OVER VOICE: You think his marriage bed will be delightful?

JANE: No, but at least I will experience one.

---

[9] Ibid

VOICE OVER VOICE: How could it compare to the good times we have together?

JANE: I would like the chance to discover how—

VOICE OVER VOICE: You know you must refuse him.

JANE: Am I to have no rest tonight? My God, look at that! The first sliver of dawn!

VOICE OVER VOICE: If you accept him, then you will never rest again—

>(Jane and Voice Over Voice wrestle in the bedsheets and out the door, shouting, yes, no, yes, no, yes no?)

VOICE OVER VOICE: You will never rest again—

PACKING (2)
For Kate Weiss

>(Woman is packing. Her mother enters.)

MOTHER: I hear they don't have hand cream there. I brought you some.

WOMAN: Thanks mom. *(she chucks it into the suitcase.)*

MOTHER: What have you got in there?

WOMAN: FBI statistics.

MOTHER: Whatever for?

WOMAN: 50% of women are raped at home, 50% are raped in the street.

MOTHER: Oh, honey, you're not the kind of girl who should pack that.

(Woman starts to pull it out of the suitcase, reconsiders.)

WOMAN: Means I can go. Might as well. In the open road, you can run in all directions. At home, you're kinda trapped. I'll send you some postcards.

(Woman kisses her Mother. Mother holds Woman a bit too tightly, a bit too long. Woman exits. Mother stares into space, frightened.)

MOTHER: Lock the door, behind you. Please.

(Sound of a giant lock being turned.)

PHRASE BOOK
For Inês Terra

(There is a café, in Greenwich Village, NYC, where couples from many countries stare into each other's eyes, with love and longing. They do not speak each other's language.
João and Hilda stare into each other's eyes, with the beauty and longing of every poem ever written. Then they try to speak.)

HILDA: I want to speak words of English love. "I think you are hot. Will you come home with me."

JOÃO: *(flips through book)* "You must treat me with more respect."

HILDA : "Do you have STD?"

JOÃO: No. Hilda, that is not…"romantic."

HILDA: "You come here often?"

JOÃO: Not "romantic."

HILDA: "What is your sign?"

JOÃO: "Stop sign."

HILDA: I not understanding.

JOÃO : Is not "romantic."

HILDA: Okay, okay. "You are hot."

JOÃO: "Shall I open a window?"

HILDA: "Only if you wear a condom."

(They collapse with laughter, reading the phrase book.)

Writing Star II

(Radiant famous author tries to play her guitar for the audience but is constantly interrupted.)

GROUPIE ONE: How did you meet Brad Pitt?

GROUPIE TWO: Spike Lee?

GROUPIE THREE: OPRAH!!?

(The groupies overlap in a percussive, musical way.)

GROUPIE ONE: BradPittBradPittBradPittBradPittBradPittBradPitt—

GROUPIE TWO: SpikeLeeSpikeLeeSpikeLeeSpikeLeeSpikeLeeSpikeLeeSpikeLee—

GROUPIE THREE: OprahOprahOprahOprahOprahOprahOprahOprahOprahOprah—

(They end in a huge, explosive crescendo of desire.)

GROUPIE TWO: Eeeeeeeeeeeeeeeeeeeeeeeeeee!

GROUPIE THREE: Aaaaaaaaaaaaaaaaaaaaaaaaaaah!

GROUPIE ONE: IT! IT! IT!

FAMOUS AUTHOR: You've got to find your own greatness.

GROUPIE ONE: Huh?

GROUPIE TWO: What?

FAMOUS AUTHOR: You can find your own people in your own life.

GROUPIE ONE: Huh?

GROUPIE TWO: What?

FAMOUS AUTHOR: There could be a Spike Lee in your life, a friend that you could work with but you might be overlooking him or her because you are worried about meeting Spike Lee, as I did, which was a different time and place.

GROUPIE ONE: Huh?

GROUPIE TWO: What?

GROUPIE ONE: I still want to meet Brad Pitt.

GROUPIE TWO: Spike Lee!

GROUPIE THREE: There is only one Oprah!!

FAMOUS AUTHOR: *(sighs)*

FLOWERS OF YELLOW AND GREEN TOWERING OVER YOUR HEAD
Las Vegas, Nevada.

HOPE: Are they glass?

PROMISE: Yes. Chihuly.

HOPE: Chi-what?

PROMISE: He's a famous artist.

HOPE: Don't be pretentious.

PROMISE: I'm not.

HOPE: You are. Chihuly. That sounds pretentious.

PROMISE: Why? Because I know who he is and you don't?

HOPE: It's stupid.

PROMISE: What is?

HOPE: Having glass in a garden. Over our heads. It'll kill us.

PROMISE: I'm sure it's secure.

HOPE: How do you know?

PROMISE: Lawsuits.

HOPE: The honeymoon is over.

PROMISE: It just began.

HOPE: You're belittling me, lording things over me, you used to say everything I said was a delight, all my words came off "trippingly on the tongue…"

PROMISE: That wasn't me.

HOPE: Who was it then?

PROMISE: Shakespeare.

HOPE: Oh.

PROMISE: Trippingly on the tongue. That doesn't even sound like me.

HOPE: Why did you marry me? Don't you think I'm smart?

PROMISE: Do you like these shades?

HOPE: Oh no. I'm not that type of woman.

PROMISE: What are you talking about?

HOPE: The type of woman who can be distracted—oo, those shades are cool.

PROMISE: Sometimes distraction is the only way. It is! Look at those glass flowers through these shades.

HOPE: They're flowers of yellow and green towering over your head.

> *(They nod, appreciatively, then touch fingers.)*

PROMISE: Distract me.

> *(Hope nods. She kisses Promise.)*

MR. DARCY

VOICE OVER VOICE: She sits—she writes—she—

JANE: Excuse me, would you play Mr. Darcy? He is one of my characters, and he eludes me.

VOICE OVER VOICE: Of course. Delighted.

> *(Voice Over Voice/ Mr. Darcy takes Jane by the hand, begins waltzing with her.)*

JANE: Ah—dancing!

MR. DARCY/VOICE OVER VOICE: Yes. But I hate to dance. Especially in the country. *(drops her hand)*

JANE: Oh, Mr. Darcy. Alack. You elude me.

(He moves away, hides behind a pillar. Jane chases him. He runs. Jane chases. Hide and seek throughout lines below.)

JANE: How does it feel to have a fortune?

MR. DARCY/VOICE OVER VOICE: The question is impertinent.

JANE: To give bad advice?

MR. DARCY/VOICE OVER VOICE: To what do you refer?

JANE: To be more refined, more worldly than the country?

MR. DARCY/VOICE OVER VOICE: How do you think it feels?

JANE: Damn you, Mr. Darcy!

MR. DARCY/VOICE OVER VOICE: Language!

JANE: I know so little of you. Neither does--- Elizabeth Bennett. The very point. *(She stops chasing, and sits at her small, small writing desk and writes. Mr. Darcy/Voice over Voice reads over her shoulder and chuckles. Jane finishes her thought, rises, removes a glove slowly, sexily revealing her naked hand. She lays it on Darcy's cheek and looks deeply into his eyes. He melts into her touch.)*

JANE: Ah, you have a sister. And she was hard done by. So you know how 'tis.

(He nods and trembles at her understanding. They search each other's eyes.)

JANE: How 'tis. *(They kiss.)*

LOSE YOUR REPUTATION

(Daughter wants to play a board game.)

GIRL: Let's play "lose your reputation!"

MAMA: Oh, honey, I'm tired.

GIRL: Pleeeeeeease!!?

MAMA: Okay, okay, get it out…oh, honey, not the 17th century edition. Let's play 21st century edition. The game lasts longer.

GIRL: Pleeeeease? 17th century edition. Pleeeease!?

MAMA: Okay— *(rolls dice, moves her piece)*. Oh, god, I've already lost. "Suspected of cheating on husband. Stoned to death."

GIRL: My turn! My turn! What does it say?

MAMA: Oh no. "Suspected loss of virginity--"

GIRL: What's that?

MAMA: Honey, this game is too old for you.

GIRL: Pleeeeeease? What's it say, what's it say—

MAMA: "Become a prostitute, die in gutter."

GIRL: I've lost. Whaaa!

MAMA: I lost first!

GIRL: Oh. Yay! Go again. *(she rolls dice, moves playing piece)* One, two, three...what's it say, what's it say?

MAMA: You've landed in the woman writer bog.

GIRL: Yay!

MAMA: Ooo--half of your works will be destroyed because you might lose—

GIRL: Lose your reputation! Cool!

MAMA: Yeah, well, I suppose it could be worse... Oh look...you've won—

GIRL: What's it say, what's it say?

MAMA: An Aphra Behn collectable card.

GIRL: Who's she?

MAMA: 17th century woman playwright. First woman to make a living from her pen...

17th Century O

(Aphra Behn. In bed. In Antwerp. With a lover.)

LOVER: Aphra, you are quick.

APHRA: I could be slow. Or do you like me quick?

LOVER: By quick, I mean you are my match. We spar.

APHRA: Aye. *(smiles, kisses him)* With you, I am a nun who escapes her convent—

LOVER: Aphra, you are hardly a nun—

APHRA: Why thank you. When you tell me of your life, you extend me—I roam the streets in boots and a rapier--

LOVER: You are a mistress of many tricks—

APHRA: A mistress who falls but must not-- love—

LOVER: Never let your opponent see your weak spot. Never reveal your love before your lover does.

APHRA: Of course not.

TELL[10]

(Emily and Susie at their windows.)

EMILY: "Will you let me come dear Susie—looking just as I do, my dress soiled and worn--"[11]

---

[10] *Please Note: This play was originally written where "Man" was played by "Mabel," Emily Dickinson's sister-in-law. This is a version for when the play is performed with 2 women and 2 men. Please contact the author for the "Mabel" version.*

[11] Smith, Martha Nell and Hart, Ellen Louise, editors, *Open Me Carefully: Emily Dickinson's Intimate Letters to Susan*

(Susie nods and reaches out. Emily buries her head in her bosom.)

EMILY: "I am so glad dear Susie—that our hearts are always clean and always neat and lovely, and not to be ashamed--"[12]

MAN *(offstage, V.O.)*: Emily Dickinson. Spinster. All in white lace. Alone. Locked in your tower. I am your editor. I will arrange your estate. I will destroy your poems to Susie. *(Susie trembles.)*

EMILY: You cannot destroy my life.

MAN *(offstage, V.O.)*: No, but I will arrange you after death, which is all anyone will know of your life. Susie, 'tis time to wed.

EMILY: No, no, no. Susie, don't marry him.

SUSIE: Don't you love him? He is your brother.

EMILY: Not enough to let him have you.

SUSIE: Emily, it's the only way we can be together. For always and always.

EMILY: I'll look out my window and see your windows. Glass. Certain slants of light. Is this all I am to have, the pain of knowing my brother is nestled 'gainst your breast? Susie, see my body—touch me—
    (A bell rings. Susie rises to exit.)

Huntington Dickinson
[12] Ibid

EMILY: Don't marry him Susie. Don't. Is the only time you are to see my body entire is when you wash it for death?

MAN: *(entering)* Yes. Come along Susie. *(reaches out his hand. Susie takes it. Emily clings to her desperately. Susie disentangles herself, exits.)* 'Tis time to wed.

EMILY: "Tell all the truth, but tell it slant."[13]

IT'S THERE

WOMAN: I want to see it.

MAN: Why?

WOMAN: Look at it!

MAN: You don't go in it.

WOMAN: Sometimes I do.

MAN: Not often.

WOMAN: No.

MAN: What's the difference?

WOMAN: It sparkles.

MAN: Everything sparkles in the sun. But in the rain…

WOMAN: I want to hear it lap, watch it spray, feel it's mist in the air, see it stretching out in all directions.

---

[13] Dickinson, Emily, *Poems*

MAN: There are days you barely gave it a glance.

WOMAN: I knew it was there.

PAWN (17ᵗʰ Century O, Part 2)
For Thrasso Petras

(*Aphra Behn, in bed, with a lover, in Antwerp.*)

LOVER: O, Aphra…

APHRA: The cost of every expense in Antwerp is shocking. I've pawned the last of my jewelry. We're trapped.

LOVER: Do we have enough for dinner?

APHRA: 'Fraid not.

LOVER: O. Doesn't the spy business pay?

APHRA: Horribly.

LOVER: Why do you do it? You should stick with writing.

APHRA: Killigrew, my rival playwright, said I was brilliant. I was flattered. He said spying for the King would be exciting. And profitable. Everything he said was a lie.

LOVER: Darling, you are brilliant. And spying does sound exciting.

APHRA: I spy on bankers.

LOVER: O.

APHRA: Killigrew convinced me to spy for the crown because he wanted me, another playwright, out of England. Now he has the stages all to himself. Lace me up, would you?

LOVER: No. I like you like that.

APHRA: Please. Or I'll have to get the neighbor.

LOVER: Where's your maid?

APHRA: I can't afford one.

LOVER: Can't you lace your self?

APHRA: Darling, I'm no contortionist.

LOVER: Yes, you are. *(he starts to lace her up)* We could borrow money from Angellica.

APHRA: Who?

LOVER: My lover. I told you about her.

APHRA: Get out.

LOVER: Darling—

APHRA: You are a ROVER!

LOVER: Of course I am.

APHRA: Out!

LOVER: Where do you think I got my techniques?

APHRA: Out! *(he exits)* I knew he was with her and her and her...but could I restrain myself, oh no. My body is the ROVER. I had to partake. Business. Business. *(about to write, with a quill, thinking it through)* "Dear Killigrew, I hear wondrous things of your new play--" No, I cannot escape this trap in my own size. I must shrink. *(writes)* "Dear Killigrew, you know how great a child I am in other matters, I shall mind diligently what I am now about."[14] I will use this quill and write—my way—out—write my way out.

THERE IS MORE IN HEAVEN AND EARTH
for Brian Bauman and Mac Wellman

(Mama writing on the small, small writing desk. Daughter enters, puts a shoe on a plate.)

MAMA: Don't, honey.

GIRL: Why not?

MAMA: It's dirty.

GIRL: Why?

MAMA: It's the relationship. Sacred. Profane. Dirty. Clean. Relationship. Like you and me. *(gets idea, writes)* Am I your container so you can explore whatever it is you need to explore?

---

[14] From Aphra Behn's letters to Thomas Killigrew, Todd, Janet M. *The Secret Life of Aphra Behn*

GIRL: *(puts plate on shoe)* Container. For what?

MAMA: *(referring to plate on shoe)* Better. Container. I'll contain the stuff that needs to be done so you can fly.

GIRL: Fly? Yay!

MAMA: Relationship as adventure. As safety? Or inheritance-

GIRL: What is inheri-dance?

MAMA: It's—what I—give you.

GIRL: Like a present?

MAMA: Kind of.

GIRL: Like Sponge Bob? Wedding Barbie?

MAMA: Like stories.

GIRL: Or money?

MAMA: Well. Yes. *(gets idea, writes)* If we can't re-invent ourselves. We will forever be on our own planets with their own times, their own gravities—

>   *(Girl, sneakily, puts shoe back on plate.*
>   *Mama catches her, they laugh.)*

DEATH
For Debbe Gervin

>   *(Jane exhausted, gaunt. Death, who looks much like*
>   *Mr. Darcy and the Voice Over Voice, holds her tight.)*

JANE'S NIECE: Aunt Jane—

JANE: Caroline—

JANE'S NIECE: Why don't you come to the park? We could converse as my children play, discuss the war—

JANE: We lose too many men to it, my brother—*(she is stopped by a body ache)*

JANE'S NIECE: Died. In the wars. I know. Your thoughts always illuminate the dim corners of my mind—a rare pleasure when one spends ones' day with young children—

JANE: My dear Caroline, you have a noble mind—*(another pain)*

JANE'S NIECE: Dear Jane, can I make you more comfortable? *(she shakes her head)* We could discuss marriage—

JANE: The bargain of class, economics, love, and character, over time, plus time, plus time—the revelations only time can bring *(Death squeezes her tighter)*. I cannot—breathe—

JANE'S NIECE: O, Aunt Jane. I'll fetch someone—*(she runs, turns back to squeeze her hand)*. I finally read one of your books—in the chinks of my day—Aunty Jane, to see…to hear… a woman write—

JANE: *(gasps)* Thank you. *(she sounds as though she is drowning. Her lungs fill with fluid.)*

JANE'S NIECE: I'll get someone.

DEATH: I am your last love, Jane.

JANE: And only. If only we could—make more stories.

DEATH: They will do, Jane.

JANE: I am young! And cannot—

DEATH: Fate is fate, Jane.

JANE: You steal all from me—the pleasure of my niece's company, the beauty of her children—

DEATH: Fate is fate.

JANE: If I succumb to your embrace *(struggles)* allow your caress—

DEATH: Aye. That will be all.

JANE: No.

DEATH: Jane, dear Jane.

> *(At last, she looks into his eyes, lets go, dies. Caroline enters, touches her, cries. Death carries off Jane. Caroline stays where Jane's body once was.)*

US TOO

A: I can't remember it. It was glorious, all consuming. I followed it. Without question. Because I knew. My life was better with you in it. All the challenges—made me bigger, better.

B: Hullo. I'm right here.

A: *(nods)*

B: Why do you keep using the past tense?

A: Is it present?

B: No.

A: What happened?

B: It. It finally happened.

A: That thing they warned us about—

B: It's like a plant we couldn't water.

A: Why couldn't we?

B: Time. Money. Lack thereof.

A: Oh, yes.

B: Now it's dead. Could get another. Plant. Not with someone else. With you.

A: But the old one. I loved it. How do we know we'll take care of the new one?

B: *(shrugs)*

A: If I'd have known, I could have slipped a memory into a pocket.

B: You did.

A: What?

B: This poem.

A: You saved it?

B: You wrote it to me.

A: *(reading)* Oh. Oh. Yes.

> *(They smile.)*

HOLES

> *(Jane's nephew, Edward, reading letters
> (by Jane Austen). He giggles.)*

EDWARD: O! Auntie Jane!

> *(Edward resumes reading. Shakes his head, withdraws
> a pair of small, elegant scissors and begins to
> carefully cut out an offending phrase.)*

EDWARD: O.O.O, my. This will never do.

(The ghost of Jane enters. Edward continues to cut the letters with a little pocket knife. Jane as Ghost dances. Jane's niece enters.)

JANE'S NIECE: Edward! What are you doing?!!

EDWARD: Ensuring the future for our Auntie Jane. If we do not clean these letters up, she will be seen as immoral.

JANE'S NIECE: Why is this immoral?

EDWARD: Novels themselves are considered immoral…for a woman to be the author…she must be seen as beyond reproach. Remember the stories she used to tell us when we were children?

JANE'S NIECE: Yes. Oh yes.

EDWARD: Should we keep this pleasure to ourselves or share the gift of Auntie Jane's wit and invention?

JANE'S NIECE: Let her work stand as it is.

EDWARD: I wish I could. I was instructed to do this by her publisher.

(Jane's Niece grabs the snippets of paper, stuffs them in her dress.)

EDWARD: The ink will stain your skin. Your sweat will destroy the words.

JANE'S NIECE: I care not! Let me smear my body with her words. Let my skin drink them in, let them feed my heart, and I will feed my daughter's heart and she her daughter's heart…and Jane's messy soul will live on, making us laugh—

EDWARD: What would you have me do? Don't you want her to be published?

JANE'S NIECE: Is it so very bad?

EDWARD: Read.

JANE'S NIECE: *(reads, laughs)* I suppose this does not do her credit.

EDWARD: See?

JANE'S NIECE: It might be misinterpreted.

EDWARD: Misconstrued.

JANE'S NIECE: These were her private thoughts, to Cassandra. Not meant for public—

EDWARD: Consumption. *(he hands her a pair of scissors)*

(She hesitates, then joins him in cutting.)

JANE'S NIECE: We will say of events, her life was singularly...

EDWARD: Barren.

JANE'S NIECE: Yes, perfect. Barren.

PLAY TODAY 3

GIRL: Is Polly Pocket in the Village?

MAMA: Oh, honey. Let's not talk about her, you'll only get—

GIRL: Polly? Polly! What can't I play with her? Why can't she be in the village—

MAMA: She's been recalled. Honey, we've been over this, a hundred—Lead paint. She could make you sick.

Magnets, Children swallowed them and they perforated the—uh. She hurt kids. She didn't mean to.

GIRL: I miss her!

MAMA: I know. I especially loved her magnetic outfits, I wish it was so easy for Mama to get dressed and go—go! Oh god, we'll play when I get home—*(mounts bike)*

GIRL: What's your play about today?

MAMA: Love. I love you.

GIRL: I love you too.

MAMA: What's your play about today?

GIRL: I don't know.

MAMA: That's a great start.

<u>THE END</u>

Mariela Aragón Chiari as Roxana, Maritza Vernanza as Pipa in !Zapatos! (Quality: the Shoe Play), Translated by Myrna Castro, Directed by Ted Gregory, Estudio Lagartija, Panamá City, Panamá,
photo: Ted Gregory, courtesy of ELATE (Educational Latin American Theatre Exchange)

QUALITY: THE SHOE PLAY
By Elaine Avila

Recipient, "New Works for Young Women" Award," Tulsa University, Oklahoma, 2006-2007

For Rose Avila

Characters:

Roxanne, (Manager of Tremendulo Shoe Boutique)

Pippa, (hoping to be employed)

Casting Note: Actors of any ethnicity can play these roles.

Setting:

Tremendulo Shoe Boutique, The City

Tremendulo shoes are extreme works of 'art' that cost as much as shoes can cost.

Notation:
∧∧∧∧∧

Indicates a big transition or change, which can be done with or without taking a pause.

Special Thanks: Suzan-Lori Parks for guiding me into the grit, Karin Coonrod for Scaparelli Pink and Shakespearean nefariousness, Janet Sonenberg for showing me how to work with dreams, Bill Peters for the fantastic, Terrence McFarland for tales of the Manhattan fashion world over Jamba Juice, Tanja Raaste for wearing her shiny patent leather red Italian sandals, Celeste Den for her passionate precision, Dodie Montgomery, Kevin Elder, Erik Ehn, Michael Wright, Jenna T. Harris, Claire Ludwig, Carol-Anne Rennick, and Wendell Summers, R. Michael Gros, Jeanette Farr, Judy Frost, PCPA TheatreFest, Kathleen Weiss, Kerry Davidson, Suzie Payne, Stevie Miller, Micheal Vonn, Stephanie Berkmann, Sue Elworthy, Kim Tough, Susan Solt, Cindy Im, Kat Oschner, Carol Bixler, Max Truax, Brian Bauman, Sigrid Gilmer, Jen Tseui, Patty Cachapero, Rose, John, Winona Avila, Bill Clark, the members of the "Loving the Living Playwright" –Suzan-Lori Parks' class at Calarts, the members of the University of Alberta alternative dramaturgy class.

Canadian Premiere: Gravity Pope Shoes, in Edmonton, AB, Canada June 2007
Produced by Vault: Theatre of Invention
Directed by Kathleen Weiss
Tracy Penner.................Pippa
Melissa Thingelstad..........Roxanne

U.K.Premiere: Tracey Neuls Shoes, London, England, September 2007
Produced by Tanja Rasste, Nordic Nomad Productions
Directed by Kathleen Weiss
Tracy Penner.................Pippa
Melissa Thingelstad..........Roxanne

U.S. Premiere: Terra Firma, Albuquerque, New Mexico, April 2010
Produced by Tricklock Company
Directed by Kathleen Weiss
Summer Olsson.................Pippa
Elsa Menendez..........Roxanne

Central American Premiere: Estudio Lagartija, Panamá
City, Panamá, July 2012
Translated by Myrna Castro (title: *!Zapatos!*)
Directed by Ted Gregory
Mariela Aragon Chiari ...Roxana
Maritza Vernanza ....Pipa

Showcase Readings: San Francisco, CA, with Diana Boos as Pippa, Cristina Anselmo as Roxanne, at American Conservatory Theatre School, directed by the author; Seattle, WA, with Kathy Hsieh as Pippa/Roxanne; Molly Lyons as Roxanne/Pippa at SIS Productions, directed by the author; Vancouver, BC with Suzie Payne as Roxanne and Lopa Sirca as Pippa, directed by Kathleen Weiss; Albuquerque, NM with Catherine Haun as Roxanne and Danielle Louise Reddick as Pippa at the Andaluz Hotel, directed by Kathleen Weiss: Los Angeles, CA, with Celeste Den as Roxanne and Cindy Im as Pippa, directed by Karin Coonrod

Workshops: California Institute of the Arts, Los Angeles; Tulsa University, Oklahoma; University of Alberta, Edmonton, Alberta

"Girls have competitive and territorial impulses towards other girls and women. But since we lack rituals to contain open conflict, we remain reluctant to explore this mine field in sisterhood's garden."

—Naomi Wolf

"Labor is blossoming or dancing where
The body is not bruised to pleasure soul
Nor beauty born of its own despair…"

--William Butler Yeats

Scene One: Matching

Early morning. Fall.

(Pippa, outside Tremendulo Shoe Boutique. There is something a little 'off' about her clothing, as if her body were crooked and her clothes were straight. Pippa sees Roxanne, the Manager of Tremendulo Boutique, pacing, radiant with confidence, a lioness on her plot of land. Pippa watches Roxanne for a moment, takes a deep breath to get her confidence, then rings the exotic sounding bell. Roxanne assesses her from head to toe, buzzes Pippa in.)

ROXANNE: Come in, come!

(Pippa removes her coat with difficulty, surreptitiously attempts to straighten her clothes. Roxanne hands Pippa a shoe box.)

ROXANNE: Let's see how you do.

(Pippa kneels at Roxanne's feet with a Geisha like precision. Roxanne approves. Pippa turns away from Roxanne, opens the box as if it might contain a wonder of the universe. She picks up the shoe reverently. It is lighter than she imagined. Her body takes flight when she holds the shoe, which she protects as if it were a tiny bird. Gingerly, she examines the shoe's white curlicues and delicate straps. Roxanne dangles her feet out limply. Pippa struggles to take the shoes off Roxanne's passive feet.)

PIPPA: *(about to put on the shoe, stops herself)* God, I'm nervous. I've heard so much about you.

ROXANNE: What have you heard?

PIPPA: That you have exacting principles.

ROXANNE: Who did you hear that from?

PIPPA: Capitalini's, Oregamo's--I've been applying to all the best shops—

ROXANNE: Did you talk to Donatello? He thinks I'm too strict.

PIPPA: I prefer to think of it as high standards.

ROXANNE: *(clapping her hands together in delight)* Me too!

> *(Pippa makes two false starts, then carefully puts the shoes on Roxanne.)*

PIPPA: Tell me if they are too tight. Ah.. No need to stand--some shoes are more admirable when seated. Take a good look. From the side. Yes! Aren't they exquisite?

ROXANNE: Ah, Come un bacio d'aria. ...a kiss of air. We generally advise new clients away from the highest heels. They don't believe they can walk in them. Of course they can walk in them. They are perfectly designed. Women are more timid than they used to be. ^^^^Try out your patter.

PIPPA: Patter?

ROXANNE: Conversational technique. *(still seated, she grabs another pair)* Say I was eyeing these. What would you say?

PIPPA: Planning for a late summer holiday or a debutante ball?

ROXANNE: It's not late summer. I hate euphemism.

PIPPA: I'm sorry.

ROXANNE: It's Fall! Fall! Fall! ^^^^ Debutante? You think I could be a debutante?

PIPPA: Of course you could. You've got great bones.

ROXANNE: No, no, no.

PIPPA: Too medical? Too technical? Too plastic surgery?

ROXANNE: Too macabre. Too 1940s. Great bones? No-one speaks like that any more. What rock did you crawl out from under?

PIPPA: I was raised by my grandmother—

ROXANNE: No! No! No, personal details, PLEASE. The question was rhetorical. Clients never want to know a thing about you dear, even if they ask. ^^^^ Whatever your name is, I have to get back to work. Take it off.

PIPPA: Pippa. Pippa Jones. I'd love to work for you.

ROXANNE: Your look is all wrong. We prefer the simple. Handmaiden. Nondescript but expensive.

PIPPA: I can change.

ROXANNE: Oh, darling, we all think we can change.

PIPPA: ^^^^Isn't there anything I can do?

ROXANNE: I can't see that you have anything to offer. Hmm. Excuse me. My phone is vibrating. *(glancing at the caller ID)* Ah, Hildesheim. Husband must be out of town. *(Roxanne begins looking at a client file card for Hildesheim's husband's name.)* Frank. *(She picks up the on phone)* Darling Hilda! How *are* you? Face healing? Oh, darling. Think of your face lift like… re-decorating your living room. Terribly inconvenient, but it must be done. It's the perfect time to do it. With *Frank* out of town. Shall I put you down for the new collection? *(laughs)* All twenty pairs? Ah. Marvelous. *(Roxanne begins making sympathetic, syncopated sound that continue as Pippa speaks quietly.)*

PIPPA: Twenty-pairs, at $500 and up, that's $10,000 minimum in less than two minutes…*(in awe)*

ROXANNE: *(Roxanne continues sympathetic sounds, looks up, covers receiver, to Pippa)* Don't be hanging about.

> *(Pippa feels desperate, but knows it must be measured. She reaches deep inside herself for something that would move Roxanne. She picks up a shoe. Roxanne is flipping through her notes on Hilda Hildesheim. Pippa 'channels' the fantasy behind the shoe.)*

PIPPA: I am… Jacqueline Bouvier Kennedy. My shoe choices shape diplomacy. In Germany, Jack is deadlocked in negotiations with Soviet Premier Nikita Khrushchev until Khrushchev sees me, in an understated, modest black v-necked dress with elbow length sleeves and matching, boxy, low-heeled court shoes. Khrushchev takes me by the arm, charmed. I wear a pale orange silk dress in India, with dyed to match pumps...five hundred people, across the river, see me. A tiny bright dot, I am the symbol of hope, of economic prosperity, of feminine strength and sophistication, of time spent on every gracious detail, of matching.

(Pippa is shaken from her vision. Roxanne notices something is amiss.)

ROXANNE: *(to phone)* Excuse me Hilda. *(covering phone)* What?

(Pippa finds a shoe and a matching handbag, holds them out to Roxanne.)

PIPPA: What about matching?

ROXANNE: Matching?

PIPPA: Yes. Like Jacqueline Kennedy.

ROXANNE: *(she starts to cry, her throat chocked with emotion)* Matching. My mother—was a single mother. She raised us three kids on a measly secretarial pay check. We were...frugal. The only time I ever saw her spend a penny on herself was when she bought a pair of shoes and a matching handbag. I'd never seen her so happy. Matching. However did you make me remember that? Matching. *(Roxanne is utterly captivated, feeling her body transform into towering wisdom and grace. She could be a mentor to this young woman.)* You are a charming girl. Intuitive. *(remembering Hildesheim)* Oh Hildy! Forgive me! When is *Frank* back? *(whispered to Pippa.)* Come back tomorrow. 8 a.m. I'll give you a bit of training, see how you do. *(to Hildy)* He didn't. Oh. Oh.

PIPPA: *(hushed, reverential)* Thank you!

ROXANNE: This is no job offer. I merely want to see if you blossom under my tutelage. *(she shuttles Pippa out of the store, makes sympathetic sounds to Hildy)* He did not. Oh how terrible!

PIPPA: Understood. Thank you.

ROXANNE: I'm not paying you for this. *(to Hildy))* Mmm. Uhhmm. Oh, sweetie. *(laughing)* Shoes always fit. *(laughs)* We're all set them Hildy? Toodaloo.

Scene Two: Instinct

*(Pippa re-enters with a large cup of coffee, dressed like Roxanne was yesterday. She
reaches in her handbag and pulls out a small motivational book and reads aloud.)*

PIPPA: *(from book)* Mary Jo was a single mother of four, on welfare. Now she is a millionaire. She turned her hobby of stamp collecting into a highly profitable business selling collectibles on Mebay. How did she do it? Desire. *(reverently)* Desire.

(Roxanne arrives. Pippa holds out the coffee.)

ROXANNE: Thank you, but I only drink—

PIPPA: Hazelnut skim latte. Double shot.

ROXANNE: *(she takes a sip)* Hmm. ^^^ You've improved your clothing. Nondescript. Come here my pretty. You said you were interviewing at Capitalini's and Oregamo's. Did you look around?

PIPPA: Of course.

ROXANNE: What did you see?

PIPPA: Are you asking me to be a mole?

ROXANNE: Did you see their upcoming collections?

PIPPA: They went over them with me.

ROXANNE: How high were the heels? How many in comparison to flats? Any boots? Open toed pumps or closed?

PIPPA: Hmm.

ROXANNE: What did you see? A few images.

PIPPA: I can't tell you that!

ROXANNE: Do you realize how difficult it is to get a job here?

PIPPA: Completely. Ms. Miller—

ROXANNE: Call me Roxanne. *Please.*

PIPPA: Roxanne. Terrific name.

ROXANNE: Thank you. Thank you. Between you and me. I hear a rumor Capatalini took a trip to the Southwest. Now he's obsessed with green chile and spiritual experiences. The word is…he's trying to capture the New Mexico quality of light in a shoe. How?[15] *(Pippa shrugs her shoulders)* Pippa, darling. I've been interviewing other girls. They were much more forthcoming.

PIPPA: If I tell you, you might hire me because I've confided in you. Or...you might find me completely untrustworthy.

ROXANNE: Did you see them? Do you remember?

PIPPA: Of course I remember. *(pause. She says nothing.)*

ROXANNE: ^^^Clever girl. We must have no leaks in a creative business like ours. Tremendulo's designs must be a surprise the day they are unveiled, or else... all we are selling is shoes.

PIPPA: And we are selling the zeitgeist of the moment.

ROXANNE: You've been reading our web page.

PIPPA: Of course.

ROXANNE: We aren't selling the zeitgest of the moment. We sell the zeitgest of before the moment. We are selling being ahead of fashion, giving the woman the illusion that she is a maker of fashion. How would you sell these?

---

[15] There are different jokes about Maximo's travels for the Canadian, British and Panamanian productions, please contact the author for details.

PIPPA: Gladiators. They lace up the calf in the most provocative way. They are about women who still care about looking fantastic.

ROXANNE: All you are showing me is that you can memorize our website. Parrots can memorize.

PIPPA: Do you want my resume? References?

ROXANNE: No. That is so working class. You've got to get out of budget thinking. Answer me this. It's the most basic question of all questions: Why would a woman buy the best shoes in the world? Cost be damned.

PIPPA: Status. Craftsmanship. Style.

ROXANNE: More specific. Feeling. She's married. For twenty years.

PIPPA: Nostalgia? Romance.

ROXANNE: Not good enough Miss Jones. ∿∿∿ I've got to open the store now—

PIPPA: Revenge? Revenge.

ROXANNE: Very good. Why revenge?

PIPPA: She thought her husband was a gentleman, a prince, and she helped him build his career, but now, he makes these little digs at her. She's raising his children but she doesn't have a "real job," so she… buys the most expensive shoes she can, hoping he will notice her, but if he doesn't, at least she is sticking it to him in a way he can say nothing about—

ROXANNE: Not bad. But you've got to go deeper. Hmm. My phone is vibrating. *(Reads ID, quick intake of breath)* It's Maximo. *(to Pippa)* I'm his muse.

PIPPA: You are?

ROXANNE: Mmm. *(she nods, answers phone)* Darling. Hello. No. The spring collection isn't quite there yet. I told you. Our clients are ready for erotic this season. They are. Mmm No, no mauve. Scaparelli pink. I know. Call that one "stimulate."

PIPPA: *(whispered)* You give him your ideas?

ROXANNE: *(nods to Pippa, speaks to Maximo)* Mmm.

PIPPA: *(whispered)* I thought he was an auteur.

ROXANNE: *(shakes her head 'no' to Pippa, speaks to Maximo)* Darling, have fun with your mama. Give her my love. Kisses. *(hangs up, speaks to Pippa)*

PIPPA: Does he give you any credit?

ROXANNE: Of course not. Pippa, if you want to be a top salesgirl, you've got to understand the women. You've got to go deeper.

PIPPA: Deeper. Deeper.

(Pippa picks up a shoe. Roxanne flips through her client files or client book. Pippa slips into her dreamworld, where she can channel the fantasy behind the shoe.)

PIPPA: Like a lioness, I pace behind the cage. All I have is instinct. A shoemaker comes and fits me for boots, that lace up my calves in the most provocative way. I beg the shoemaker to rescue me, letting my short toga fall up a little higher. Hinting at the treasures lurking higher, higher. He laughs and says he'll see me in the ring. He wants to see me wrestle, he wants to see me bleed, scratched in the dust, struggling with all my might. Watching me use everything I have, to fight to the death.

(Pippa is shaken. Roxanne notices there is something a bit odd.)

PIPPA (CON'T): Gladiators appeal to a woman who knows the power of legs. The lacing is a ladder…to treasures, higher and higher. The Gladiator woman intimately understands the link between sex and survival. Her life is precious. She fights to live. Even if it turns her into a monster, a killer, a slut.

ROXANNE: You're hired.

PIPPA: *(Pippa begins hyperventilating, as if she won a prize on a game show.)* Oh God, O God, I don't know how to thank you.

ROXANNE: Sell. Sell. Sell. That's all the thanks I'll ever need. *(she waves Pippa off.)*

Scene Three: Drive

Morning. Outside Tremendulo Boutique.

(Pippa, with the manikin foot and shoe, practicing. She slips the shoe on perfectly, repeats three times. Sits back with satisfaction on the ledge outside the shop. Finds her motivational book, reads aloud.)

PIPPA: Sally Smith annoyed her landlords for years. She could only afford tiny apartments and was frequently evicted for her collection of cats, small dogs, and hamsters. Now she owns one of the most successful pet franchises in the world. Drive. Determination. Drive. Desire. Drive. Drive.

(Roxanne enters, hands Pippa a key. Pippa holds it reverently, looks for a perfect place to put it, decides to place it on her necklace, so that it is close to her heart.)

ROXANNE: Your hair. An updo would be better. Mr. Tremendulo likes to think of our boutique as a cross between a hair salon, a lingerie store and an art gallery. Mr. Tremendulo hates
marriage-- you aren't married, are you?

PIPPA: No.

ROXANNE: Ever been married?

PIPPA: No.

ROXANNE: This is strictly out of curiosity, you understand, not a job requirement. Of course, that would be illegal. Are you serious about anyone?

PIPPA: No.

ROXANNE: Excellent. We are like brides of shoes to him, a kind of nunnery of fashion. Handmaidens. Don't gain a pound. Not one pound. We get an occasional tourist. Smile at them directly. It will intimidate them if they don't have the money to spend on the shoes. If they are too pushy, call our security guard, Ricky. Oh, there he is. *(she waves hello, she goes weak in the knees, he is a devastatingly sexy 'hunk')* Hello Ricky. *(she recovers from the sight of Ricky.)* People who aren't here to buy **must not** waste our time.....which is spent fostering *relationship*.

PIPPA: *(reverently)* Relationship.

ROXANNE: Then you can get on the phones and sell twenty at a time. You have a certain something. You know hidden things. About the shoes? How?

PIPPA: I don't know what you are talking about.

ROXANNE: Natural gifts aside. You've got to focus on the client. The women. Everyone thinks it's the shoes. But it's the women that matter. We use intimacy in the service of selling. Let's practice. I am a rich business woman with a case of dissipated ennui. I want a promotion. I'm shopping. Go. *(Roxanne pretends to be this business woman , examining shoes)* "Hmmm."

PIPPA: May I help you?

ROXANNE: Too assertive. Try again.

PIPPA: Ma'am?

ROXANNE: No. No. Women of certain age hate to be called ma'am.

PIPPA: Miss?

ROXANNE: Too spinsterish.

PIPPA: Ms.?

ROXANNE: Oh God, no.

PIPPA: I give up. What do I do?

ROXANNE: Think foreign.

PIPPA: Oh. Mademoiselle?

ROXANNE: Yes. Perfect. Signorina in a pinch. Try again. I'm shopping. I desperately need shoes that intimidate my subordinates and impress my superiors. *(as business woman)* "They see me as a function, not as a master. I need shoes to change all that." Go.

PIPPA: Mademoiselle—that feels so diminutive.

ROXANNE: It's European. It can't possibly be diminutive if it's European.

PIPPA: Mademoiselle--is there any chance you might--

ROXANNE: TOO MUCH. Didn't you see my face? You never say more than Mademoiselle and back off. And say it very sweetly, quietly, sincerely--as if you hate to interrupt my exquisite thoughts. *(as business woman)* "How can I avoid…being passed over? Again."

PIPPA: Like this? Mademoiselle--

ROXANNE: Good, good. And back off and don't look me in the eye so much.

PIPPA: Now what?

ROXANNE: I approach you.

PIPPA: Oh.

ROXANNE: More subservient. You're playing her ideal employee. So in awe of her accomplishments that you're afraid to speak. I've got to know that I can call on you at a moment's notice, but there is no way you will disturb my poignancy. Boss lady *(as businesswoman)* "Top dog. Ultimate."

PIPPA: Okay. Poignancy. Poignancy.

ROXANNE: "Miss. These. In a seven and a half."

PIPPA: Of course, signorina.

ROXANNE: What are you about to go do?

PIPPA: Get her the shoes?

ROXANNE: How many?

PIPPA: One pair?

ROXANNE: No. No. No. Options. You must bring at least four pairs. A size smaller, a size larger, and something else, something challenging. Why would a man buy shoes here?

PIPPA: For himself? A drag show? No. For his mistress?

ROXANNE: Good. What mistake is he likely to make?

PIPPA: Not buying any for his wife?

ROXANNE: Don't worry about that. She'll buy ten pairs just to spite him.

PIPPA: He'll buy the wrong size?

ROXANNE: And do we correct him?

PIPPA: Yes. No?

ROXANNE: That way, the mistress will have to come in to exchange them, and she'll probably buy another pair while she's at it...on his expense account. She's got to take advantage. Before he tires of her. Next. How do you get an older woman to give up high heels? *(Roxanne pretends to be an eighty year old woman grasping at the shoes.)* "Oh--"

PIPPA: You subtlely suggest--

ROXANNE: No. No. Nothing subtle. *(as eighty-year old woman)* "Oh--"

PIPPA: You yell at her?

ROXANNE: Like a petulant child. Here, try. *(as eighty-year old woman)* "Oh...pretty--"

PIPPA: *(much too aggressively)* No. Mademoiselle. No. No heels.

ROXANNE: Not quite. Call her by her first name if you can. In this case, intimacy is more important than subservience. Then, say something her mother might have said to her. *(as eighty-year old)* "Sweet--"

PIPPA: Roxanne. Put those down. You'll break your neck. Remember the last time. How many times to I have to tell you?

ROXANNE: Very good. Clients love to be bossed around—it's one of the biggest secrets of our business. They adore being noticed. This also works with brides, but in very small doses. Pretend I'm planning a wedding. Make my agenda your own—*(she picks up a high heel, pretends to be a petulant bride)* "Oh God, The stress. The stress!"

PIPPA: Are you walking down the aisle? You'd fall on your face.

ROXANNE: Good. Small doses. Change tactics. Fast.

PIPPA: What sort of a wedding are you planning? How many guests?

ROXANNE: "Small. Five hundred. On Daddy's boat."

PIPPA: Would you like a seat? Is there any champagne I could offer her?

ROXANNE: Always keep some chilling in the back. For the brides. Goes well with the valium. She's had half a bottle.

PIPPA: What time of day is it?

ROXANNE: Valium and champagne go well together at any time of day. You offer her the champagne…*(as bride)* "I'll have a wee bit. I've just been so stressed…I had no idea weddings were so involved…"

PIPPA: Are you a tiny bit restored? Ready to see some lovely shoes? We'll go slo—w.

ROXANNE: Good. She glories in all the attention, but it overwhelms her. Soothe her, sedate her.

PIPPA: *(pours more champagne into Roxanne's glass)* Sedate her.

ROXANNE: Cheers. I raise my glass to you. Few have received my training with such determination.

PIPPA: *(whispered)* Determination.

ROXANNE: By the way, your name is fabulous. Pi—ppa. Pippa. Pippa. It makes me think of all that's good about being a girl. That bit about the gladiators. Inspired. *(a toast)* To survival.

PIPPA: To survival.

Scene Four: Holes

One Week Later. The end of the work day.

(Pippa's hair is swept into the updo Roxanne suggested, but she is defeated, dejected. She gathers her coat from the back, begins to leave.)

ROXANNE: Pippa! Time for your first employee review.

PIPPA: I can't gain a pound. Not one pound.

ROXANNE: Did you forget?

PIPPA: How do you make someone want to know you, confide in you immediately?

ROXANNE: Are you dizzy? Sit down.

PIPPA: You've got to look good, be thin. And be friendly, not too friendly.

ROXANNE: Let's take a look at your sales. Oh. Oh, dear. Pippa, your sales must go up or—

PIPPA: No--

ROXANNE: Or, Pippa, you go out.

PIPPA: No, no. Roxanne! Don't you—care?

ROXANNE: I care. I do. I've passed down my most treasured tips. But I must see the results. In sales. It's the way of the world.

PIPPA: I need more help. Please. Some say knowledge increases it's value when you pass it on.

ROXANNE: Who says that?

(Pippa holds out her self help book, Roxanne flips through it.)

ROXANNE: Stamp Collecting? Hamsters? Oh, no wonder you can't sell. *(laughing)* Pippa, this is a *general* business book. Tremendulo shoes are not "units."

PIPPA: I thought it had a few good points.

ROXANNE: This book is a crutch. Destroy it.

PIPPA: But—

ROXANNE: Destroy it.

(Pippa rips the book apart, with some difficulty. Roxanne walks on it, driving it into the carpet with her heels.)

ROXANNE: Pippa, darling, business has always had a tempestuous relationship with art. Clean it up. *(Pippa kneels and does so)* Who have you waited on?

PIPPA: Oh, various people.

ROXANNE: Pippa. Who are they?

PIPPA: There is this incredibly fat woman. It's disgusting. Her feet roll over the edges of the shoes.

ROXANNE: Weight is immaterial to a woman's worth, Pippa.

PIPPA: Why can't I gain any weight then?

ROXANNE: Them, not us.

PIPPA: She follows Mr. Tremendulo around the world like she's his lap dog.

(Roxanne brings Pippa a garbage pail to throw out the pages of her business book. Pippa does so, mournfully.)

ROXANNE: *(muttering)* Must be Babette van Buren. What hole is she trying to fill?

PIPPA: Hole? Fill? How should I know?

ROXANNE: Find out. Was she alone?

(Roxanne flips through her client files or client book. Pippa sneaks one page of the torn book for herself, and hides it in her clothes.)

PIPPA: She came in with her friend.

ROXANNE: Do a bit of her for me. *(Pippa does a physical impression of "Flora.")* Probably Flora, Flora Baldwin. Of the Baldwins who made their money in baked goods. No doubt, they were sporting their floor length furs.

PIPPA: Flora was. With a white t-shirt and jeans. As if she was slumming it. Flora said "when I dated my husband, I wore flats. Now that we're married, I wear heels so I can tower over him! Ha. Ha, ha, ha, ha." The fat woman---

ROXANNE: Don't call her that. *Please.* You've got to empathize with her.

PIPPA: Empathize. She didn't even look at the shoes." When I was in Milan last we--ek, Max-i-mo was presenting his collection, I bought half a dozen more shoes than I pla---nned. When I got home, Ja---mes--"

ROXANNE: Her husband.

PIPPA: I assume so. "Ja--mes told me he just ha---tes Mr. Tremend--u--lo. Just ha--tes him." *(Pippa does Bab's long and nasal laugh.)* Then Flora said, "buy half a dozen more pairs, and tell James, I said so."

ROXANNE: Did she?

PIPPA: No. She said. "Ja---mes would kill me." Babette absent-mindedly brushed against the most innovative...the most daring shoes...

ROXANNE: What then?

PIPPA: They left. Without buying anything.

ROXANNE: You don't believe she deserves these shoes.

PIPPA: She doesn't. She's just so...so...

ROXANNE: So--what?

PIPPA: Selfish.

ROXANNE: Babette is married to a rich alcoholic. He drinks himself into oblivion and then stumbles home and pees the bed. She's afraid all the time, of her cook, her maid—it's all staff that have been in her husband's family for years. Shoes are her only pleasure.

PIPPA: Pleasure...

ROXANNE: Tell me about the first time you wore high heels.

PIPPA: I don't remember.

ROXANNE: You were five or six...

PIPPA: My grandmother had these shiny heels lying on the carpet--

ROXANNE: You tried to walk in her footsteps--

PIPPA: I could.

ROXANNE: Everyone looked at you.

PIPPA: They did.

ROXANNE: What a rush. ^^^^Then when you were a teenager, you had to go to some god awful suburban prom, no doubt. You needed heels—

PIPPA: I didn't think I could walk in them, let alone dance.

ROXANNE: You slipped your foot into the shoe, wobbled a bit, found your balance. In one moment, you went from girl to woman. You don't know what our women go through. Their bodies are phoenixes rising from the ashes of childbirth, cancer, emotional abandonment. You judge our ladies because they are rich. But what if you could separate beauty from commerce? Then the shoes could be pure spirit. Abundance. Beauty. A celebration of womanly grace. If you understand that, your sales will go up. Remember. *Empathize.* Of course, we all have trouble with that sometimes. *(referring to a sporty pair of shoes)* Ugh. if you can discern what sort of woman would want these rubberized practicalities, you could sell anything. *(She turns to tidy a display.)*

PIPPA: Empathize.   *(Pippa picks up a shoe and decides to channel, this is in a Russian accent)* "VVVrrroooommmmm. Vvvvrooomm. Flattened by megatons of gravity..."I am Valentina Tereshkova, the first woman, the first woman in space. Men are used to see us only as their comrades, their friends. They do not see us as what we are, "a straightforward aviation engineer. My expertise is in cosmonautics and I work professionally as a scientist."[16]

(Roxanne catches Pippa in her "channeling."). We share a beautiful and small planet. We must have international collaboration. For space travel, I wear sensible yet stylish, aerodynamic shoes that bounce—bounce---bounce off the walls."

ROXANNE: PIPPA!? What are you doing?

PIPPA: I—feel the story of the shoe—these are for a woman who wants to be an astronaut.

ROXANNE: An astronaut. Oh, yes. For a woman who wants to be "one of the boys." *(She shudders)* Pippa. How did you know that? What were you doing?

PIPPA: It's a kind of shoe –

ROXANNE: Channeling.

PIPPA: Yes. That's how I knew about matching. I was Jacqueline Bouvier Kennedy. A woman gladiator. An astronaut. It's thrilling but scary.

ROXANNE: How long have you—

PIPPA: It started when I first wore my grandmother's shoes. But here, in the boutique, it's extra—

ROXANNE: Powerful.

PIPPA: Yes. There are more—

---

[16] O'Neill, Bill, "Whatever became of Valentina Tereshkova?" New Scientist, 14 August 1993

ROXANNE: Vibrations. Darling, I understand completely.

PIPPA: How?

ROXANNE: I told you. I'm Maximo's muse.

PIPPA: Wow. Does he ever come to the shop? Meet the women?

ROXANNE: He's like the sun, he's everywhere, but he's---. *(feels her phone vibrate)* Hmm. Vibration. ^^^ It's Maximo. His ears must be burning. Ha, ha. I've got to take this. Hello, love. Oh, I get tired of those kidney people. What about film restoration? Don't they have a benefit? Ooo. Maximo, even in an über-erotic collection you can turn to open heartedness. Tenderness. You can. *(Pippa sneaks another page of her book out of the garbage, hides it in her clothes.)* Yes, yes, finish up with your mother. Oh, darling. I can't wait! *(Roxanne begins gathering shoes by the armful)* Pippa, your talent is all well and good but you must connect it to your clients. The women. Now. Let's pick some shoes for Bling--

PIPPA: *Bling? Bling.* Oh my God.

ROXANNE: She's on location somewhere in Canada. *(looking through client file)* Going into simplicity these days. Might even change her name. Her new album won't even have a name. Simple. Hmm.

PIPPA: How about these?

ROXANNE: Uh. Ah. Channel them.

PIPPA: "Straw" *(she channels)* "I'm meditating. With the Dalai Lama on a simple straw mat. I've been on a week long cleanse. Only fruit, brown rice. Mineral water. I can feel the sludge of my soul sloughing off – like a spiritual loofa."

ROXANNE: No, no, no. She'll never sell a thriller about skydiving wearing those.

PIPPA: You're right. I don't know anything about her. I only feel the shoes.

ROXANNE: Don't worry. I'll do some of her for you. *(as Bling)* "5 a.m. I start with a facial, steam, microdermibrasion. Ow. My face hurts. 6a.m. to 8a.m. I work out with my personal trainer. 8 a.m. vegetable protein smoothie sent over by my dietician. God. I'm still hungry. My face hurts."

PIPPA: Why does she have to do all that? She's gorgeous.

ROXANNE: She's forty. It's no achievement to look good at twenty, but, with every passing year, the effort becomes increasingly…Herculean. Powerwalking. Kickboxing. Yogalates. Bootcamp Fatblaster.

PIPPA: *(looks at client file or book)* She exercises at least four hours a day.

ROXANNE: She can't look her real age. Or her career is…over. She'll--

PIPPA: Disappear.

ROXANNE: She needs shoes to--

PIPPA: Stand out. *(selects a shoe)* "Spectaculars!" *(channeling "spectaculars")* "I will hang like a bat, every night, if that's what it takes. I will look 20 at 60. I will never disappear. I will never be dismissed. I am Bling. Peace. I am Peace. I am Spectacular."

ROXANNE: Beautiful, Pippa. You've linked the fantasy to the client. Wrap these up, would you? Courier them to Iceland. Nunavet. Baffin Island. Whatever. I don't know. Check with her assistant. *(phone vibrates, she speaks to it, but does not answer)* I'm coming. He must be done with his mama. I've got to meet Maximo at MOXA. MOXA is having a retrospective. Teacups made out of fur. Industrial scrap metal. Toilets. That sort of thing. Everything old is new again. Ha, ha, ha.

PIPPA: You helped me understand so much. Thank you.

ROXANNE: There's only one way to thank me. Sell. *(she exits)*

PIPPA: *(gathers her book out of the garbage. Finds Roxanne's pen, writes on the scraps of paper)* It's the women, not the shoes. Beauty. Beauty. Beauty seduces us all.

Scene Five: Titilate

Two weeks later.

(Roxanne, happily humming "These Boots Were Made for Walking." Pippa enters.)

ROXANNE: I love Sunday mornings. Divinely quiet. Everyone's at brunch, church, or recovering from a hangover. ^^^^Time for your reward. What do you have there?

PIPPA: My Italian isn't the best, but-- are they-- from the shoe factory?

ROXANNE: Which means?

PIPPA: It's the Spring Collection?

ROXANNE: Yes. My clever girl. Go ahead. Rip them open. Wait. Take a moment. Remember, no-one has seen these designs. We'll be the first ones. *(Pippa begins to open)* No. Not yet. One more deep breath. Until we can't stand it another moment. Now. Now. Rip. Show me one. Ah. What's it called?

PIPPA: Stimulate.

ROXANNE: Hmm. Stim-u-late. Mmmph. Maximo has outdone himself.

PIPPA: That is your idea. He is using your ideas.

ROXANNE: I know. So what? Next.

PIPPA: This one is…"Mount"…

ROXANNE: Oh. Maximo. I love it when you go all the way. God the arch. Its so sexy--the bravado in showing so much instep—mmph. This one has to go in the window.

PIPPA: What do we do with the old ones?

ROXANNE: Throw them in the back. Next.

PIPPA: No-one wears them?

ROXANNE: No.

PIPPA: They never go on sale?

ROXANNE: Of course not. That would be lowering our market worth. Pippa, please, another pair...

PIPPA: Blush.

ROXANNE: Ah. To come back to simplicity, open-heartedness, tenderness. After feeling jaded...that is true mark of his artistry. Do several all at once--oh god, I can't stand it. *(she unwraps them too.)*

ROXANNE & PIPPA: Oh. Oh. Oh. Ah. *(Roxanne and Pippa rests, satiated.)*

ROXANNE: Pippa, be a dear and put Arouse, Envy, and Titillate in the window, would you?

> *(Pippa does so, with reverence. Pippa and Roxanne bask in a mutual glow.)*

PIPPA: Do you remember what you said? About high heels—women being too timid--

ROXANNE: Yes?

PIPPA: Let's turn that around.

ROXANNE: Sell them on boldness—

PIPPA: Defiance.

ROXANNE: The sexiness of their walk—

PIPPA: The line of their body—

ROXANNE: Can't get that with flats. Let's practice. Think of your clients…which one is most timid?

PIPPA: Art history professor. ^^^ I had one yesterday.

ROXANNE: Did she buy anything?

PIPPA: No. But she wanted to.

ROXANNE: How could she? On her salary. An inheritance?

PIPPA: No. She's the type that eats ramen. Saves up for a spectacular splurge. Once in her life.

ROXANNE: Let's get inside her head. I'll kick us off. "I am forty-five years old, somehow I missed dating. Busy in my art historical enclave, I came to know more about painting techniques of the Renaissance than about people."

PIPPA: "I have to commute two hours into the city, and still my apartment, that I can barely afford, is 25 square feet…"

ROXANNE: " I got thinner and thinner, my body—"

PIPPA: "-- a wiry artistic extension of myself—"

ROXANNE: "Silhouetted against the smart classroom projections--"

PIPPA: "My voice disembodied in the dark--"

ROXANNE: "--wispy grey hair--"

PIPPA: "Unseen--"

ROXANNE: "Flattened against the wall at art openings, smiling wanly at my more famous students— We'll get her into heels.

PIPPA: Three-inch minimum.

ROXANNE: Let's sell her. I want to do a tag team with you.

PIPPA: What do I—

ROXANNE: We play off of each other. Put the shoes there. We'll pretend it's her. Right. The watcher gauges how it's going, then moves in, we switch.

PIPPA: Signorina, may I be of assistance—

ROXANNE: She's frightened. Too much. Excuse my employee. Great glasses. I love your hair.

PIPPA: You look strong enough to tower—

ROXANNE: To saunter—

PIPPA: To sashay—

ROXANNE: All those people watching you all day, how lovely it would be to feel that every piece of your ensemble is impeccably in place--

PIPPA: She's scared—how do you know people watch her—

ROXANNE: Didn't you speak at the Blick opening? Weren't the appy's divine? How could I forget a woman of your wit--

PIPPA: --and grace?

ROXANNE: Want to try something bold?

PIPPA: How about… "titillate"?

ROXANNE: Too sexual, you're scaring her.

PIPPA: "Command."

ROXANNE: Too much.

PIPPA: She brushed against the Louis XIV fleur de lis slippers—three inch heels—just like French royalty.

ROXANNE: Good. These will make her feel substantial. Her grey hair celebrated, powdered, piled upon her head—I know. Let's channel them together.

PIPPA: Touch them. Aren't they supple? Impeccable construction. *(Pippa channels)* "I leave my four poster bed and slip into my brocade dressing gown--"

ROXANNE: *(touching shoes)* I'm there. "My entourage racing after me as I make my very important meetings regarding the commissioning of important playwrights and their tributes to me,"

PIPPA: "everyone hanging on my every word, my slightest displeasure--"

ROXANNE: "Power, arbiter of all culture. Deciding what shall happen. What shall be eaten, read, viewed, loved--"

PIPPA: "adored by the wealthiest in my realm."

ROXANNE: "Everyone follows me. I am the Queen."

PIPPA: So what if they cost a months pay?

ROXANNE: They are worth it.

PIPPA: Too high? They are designed like a cathedral. Perfectly balanced. You could stand in them all day.

ROXANNE & PIPPA: "Uh…I'll give them a try."

(They break into peals of laughter.)

ROXANNE: That was great.

PIPPA: Link her pain to a fantasy, and you have the key to her heart.

ROXANNE: Precisely.

PIPPA: Oh, Roxanne, you've climbed inside my head and thrown out all the junk. Redecorated.

Scene Six: Tag

One week later. Closing time.

(Roxanne pours herself a scotch, kicks off her heels, stretches out on a sofa. The lights of the city come out as they speak.)

ROXANNE: Pippa. Pippa. Pippa. I've turned you into our top salesgirl. With wonderful new concepts. That vintage Tremendulo idea of yours— inspired. We sell off the pairs in the back from past seasons—

PIPPA & ROXANNE: --at top prices.

ROXANNE: Pippa, you're carrying on my tradition, I'm proud. Oh, so proud.

PIPPA: *(eyes shining with tears)* Thank you.

ROXANNE: The empathy you're pumping out at our ladies--- it's turned into a terrific sales spike. Are you ready for the biggest reward of all? *(Pippa nods)*

(Roxanne pops over to her, hands her an envelope. Quiet, enthusiastic anticipation as Pippa opens and reads.)

ROXANNE (CON'T): You get to come along with me. You.

PIPPA: *(like she has won on a game show)* The trunk signing? I get to see Tremendulo personally unveil his collection. Oh, my God.

ROXANNE: Tables of champagne, stacks of pastries—

PIPPA: Of course I won't touch any of it. But to see. To see.

ROXANNE: Ah. To see the history of the women we have waited on. It's fantastic. Women bring their older

Tremendulos, cradled like children or precious love letters. Each shoe has a story...these they wore disco dancing, these they wore to the best Opera they ever heard, these they took on safari to Africa...They hold them out to Maximo to sign the bottoms, hands trembling with excitement...

PIPPA: Wait--when they walk in them--won't his signature wear off?

ROXANNE: Women encase the shoes in plexiglass.

PIPPA: They never wear them again?

ROXANNE: They are works of art. Entombed like Snow White, but for all eternity.

PIPPA: Doesn't it bother you?

ROXANNE: What?

PIPPA: Never getting to actually use what we sell?

ROXANNE: We touch great artistry every day. Darling, you've been working too hard. You're tired, that's all. Cheer up. We're off to the Trunk Signing—the grandest ball of them all. And you'll meet him. He is so wowed by your idea to sell vintage Tremendulos. I'm so proud. You should be too. Here—a few touches for the party.

(Roxanne puts a fancy scarf on Pippa, an expensive pin on herself.)

PIPPA: Thank you Roxanne.

ROXANNE: Don't mention it. *(kissing her cheek)* Pippa. Pi—ppa. PIPPA.

> *(Transition: Sounds of the trunk signing, applause, many women's happy voices.)*

Scene Seven: Everyone

After the trunk signing.

> *(Roxanne is slightly disheveled, angry.)*

PIPPA: The shiny silver escalator lifted me onto the gleaming white top floor, surrounded by the gurgle of champagne fountains, cameras flashing, Hollywood stars. And the conversationalists—The Times Style Section Editor, the publisher of French Vogue, the woman who created the phrase "toe cleavage."

ROXANNE: I had no idea you would ingratiate yourself with him. My god.

PIPPA: Mr. Tremendulo was thrilled to listen to my ideas.

ROXANNE: Tremendulos for everyone. They aren't for everyone.

PIPPA: Don't all women have the right to wear Tremendulos?

ROXANNE: The right? Pippa, Everyone can own a Picasso print, but not everyone can own an actual Picasso.

PIPPA: Access. It's the essence of free market democracy.

ROXANNE: Democracy? If our society were truly democratic, we'd be out of a job. The rich get richer and we wait on them to survive.

PIPPA: I know that. But it's not only the rich who can get richer. Don't you believe in democracy?

ROXANNE: Darling, life itself isn't democratic. Your gift, to intuit the fantasy behind the shoe, is a perfect example. Not everyone can do that.

PIPPA: Roxanne, what are you worried about? Most of the top designers have a cheap line.

ROXANNE: Not us.

PIPPA: Why not? Tremendulo could make a killing. Especially if he sold them in P-Mart and Arrow stores.

ROXANNE: God forbid. *(she takes aspirin with a shot of scotch.)* We'd be—common. Pippa, our shoes are sports cars. For women. They must be impeccably constructed.

PIPPA: Mercedes made the smart car.

ROXANNE: So make a few green, environmentally correct shoes. But make them well and sell them at top dollar. Pippa, our shoes are not units. What would your tawdry bits of access be made of? Something cheap, right? Fake leather. UGH. Blisters. Corns. Wobbles. Ugh.

PIPPA: There are many ways to lower the cost of construction.

ROXANNE: Exactly. What of the factory workers in Perugia? They are paid well for their services, and they deserve it—they have raised shoe making to a high art. Would you fire them?

PIPPA: We might have to find workers who appreciate a new opportunity--

ROXANNE: You mean the three dollar a day countries, don't you? Oh, God.

PIPPA: Mr. Tremendulo knows how to look after his own business opportunities. There is nothing stopping us from making the high end shoes in Perugia and the cheaper ones in Thailand. Or the Philippines. ^^^^
ROXANNE: Do you plan to have these cut rate, accessible scraps sold here?

PIPPA: Of course. It's the flagship store.

ROXANNE: Ridiculous. Selling $70 shoes in front of my women.

PIPPA: They don't have to look at them. We could put them in a corner.

ROXANNE: The problem, Pippa, is that you will drive out the rich. The ones who actually pay top dollar. For quality. I can't do that to my clients. They expect me to uphold a certain standard. We'd be overrun by suburbanites, commoners. I won't subject my women to that.

PIPPA: I'm already working out the details with Maximo.

ROXANNE: How dare you.^^^ I made you.

PIPPA: You made me?

ROXANNE: You were a lost little shoe fanatic. Now you are a top salesgirl at the premiere shoe boutique in the country. With an invitation to the most exclusive trunk signing in the city.

PIPPA: You made me?

ROXANNE: What were you without me?

PIPPA: Roxanne. I made myself.

ROXANNE: Pippa, none of us can get anywhere without each other. I beg you not to lower the standards of the shop. I beg you.

PIPPA: How can raising our profits be lowering our standards?

ROXANNE: Oh, Pippa, Pippa, Pippa. In a thousand ways. A thousand, thousand ways.

PIPPA: You're the one who taught me to use my gift in the service of selling.

ROXANNE: Everything is for sale dear. Even us. But there are ways to go about it, without being cheap.

Scene Eight: Women. Shoes. History.

A few days later. 7 a.m.

(Pippa sits alone. Roxanne enters.)

PIPPA: *(pulls out a coffee)* I brought you your favorite coffee, and a pastry.

ROXANNE: Keep the pastry. Eat it yourself.

PIPPA: I bought it for you.

ROXANNE: I don't eat pastry.

PIPPA: Not even as a special treat?

ROXANNE: I never eat it. Never, never.

PIPPA: How about the coffee? It has nonfat milk and zero calorie hazelnut syrup.

ROXANNE: The coffee is cold.

PIPPA: I didn't know when you'd be coming in and I wanted it to be here, I can re- heat it--

ROXANNE: No thanks. I prefer the fresh, the ready. Not coffee that's lowered its standards.

PIPPA: I could get you another.

ROXANNE: Forget it. Excuse me. *(she begins laying out little cards, setting out vintage Tremendulos.)* Carry on with whatever it is you are doing.

PIPPA: Your display looks fantastic.

ROXANNE: Thank you.

PIPPA: *(reads one of the cards)* "Women. Shoes. History." Sounds fascinating.

ROXANNE: It is.

(They work in stony silence for as long as they can stand.)

PIPPA: Is wanting everyone to have the Tremendulo experience that bad?

ROXANNE: It's an erosion.

PIPPA: Are you going to be angry with me forever? *(pause, reads a card from Roxanne's display)* Women in ancient Rome put the faces of their enemies on the insoles of their sandals so they could walk all over them.

ROXANNE: You can't keep your hands off my things, can you?

PIPPA: I miss you. We used to have such fun together. To bring in the history--it's brilliant.*(reading another card)* A contest? To win a free pair of vintage Tremendulos? If you can guess which woman in history had the most pairs of shoes? *(pause)* Imelda Marcos?

ROXANNE: Ah. She loved American culture. But no.

PIPPA: You waited on her? Of course you did.

ROXANNE: Whenever she was in town. Imelda is too contemporary. Go farther back.

PIPPA: Marie Antoinette?

ROXANNE: Hmm. Not bad. It's a tie, between her and Catherine d' Medici, who brought the first heels to France.

PIPPA: *(reading a card)* "Marie Antoinette had a maid whose only job was to organize her slippers by style, date worn, and color..." *(reads another card)* "Catherine d' Medici wore heels to be as tall as her husband for her wedding. Then everyone started wearing them, higher and higher, until the entire French aristocracy needed canes to walk down the street."

ROXANNE: Men too.

PIPPA: I'm happy for you. Why can't you be happy for me? Maximo loved my ideas. Look. *(she pulls out a sketch book).* Tremendulo drew these based on my concepts. My concepts. Women used to wear matching handbags with their shoes. These shoes ARE handbags. You can fit a lipstick, a pen, a notebook, a tampon, a credit card and a driver's license-- all in the shank of the shoe.

ROXANNE: Your ideas are tacky. Tacky.

PIPPA: Yes. But they will be hugely successful.

ROXANNE: Tell me honestly. Aren't you afraid that your cheap ideas will cheapen your gift?

PIPPA: No. I'm sellin' "it." Like you taught me. Maximo is taking my ideas, but everyone is giving me credit for it. I'm at all the meetings. His accountant kissed me on both cheeks. I swear he did.

ROXANNE: Darling, will you get me a fresh hazelnut latte? Go out the back.

(Pippa nods, angrily. Exits. Roxanne makes a sneaky phone call.)

ROXANNE (CON'T): Maximo, I'm warning you, Pippa is-- Her credentials are terrible--and her ideas—Maximo, for God's sakes! Our women count on us—what? But she isn't—well. Mentally well. She has a touch of fetishism. I caught her touching the shoes.^^Oh. Funny. *(she laughs)* Wild. Yes, I guess she is. What? Cancel ? Oh, of course, Maximo. I understand. You're busy with your mother? Not with Pippa? Your mother. Ha, ha. Darling, I have some ideas for next season—you're working with Pippa on that? Oh, of course. *(she exits, dejectedly.)*

Scene Nine: Toxic

(Pippa enters, wheeling a box on a dolly.)

PIPPA: Roxanne. The boxes have arrived. A collection based on my concept. "New Direction." Help me wheel them in. I hope you can stay late. *(Roxanne enters)* Great. ^^^ Roxanne, you may rip. Wait, a moment of anticipation--

(Roxanne does not wait. She pulls out an exacto knife and slices the box open.)

ROXANNE: Oh. Here. At last.

PIPPA: Read out the names of the shoes, please.

ROXANNE: *(dispassionately)* "Handbag." "Walk all over Me."

PIPPA: Hold them up for me to see.

ROXANNE: "Toxic."

PIPPA: You could be a little more enthusiastic.

ROXANNE: You could come up with something a little more…classic.

PIPPA: Roxanne, classic is old fashioned. My ideas are up-to-the-minute. Go on.

ROXANNE: These shoes are iPhones.

PIPPA: People take their shoes off and then talk on them. Like James Bond.

ROXANNE: Darling, you forget. Feet sweat. We don't want our phones to smell.

PIPPA: You're selling a dream, make it something everyone wants.

ROXANNE: I know how to sell.

PIPPA: Of course. You do. Only—

ROXANNE: What?

PIPPA: You could be a little bit pleased for me.

ROXANNE: Are you calling on our sisterhood? You think we're on the same side? Because we're women?

PIPPA: Roxanne, I know you don't like this concept. I had to sidestep you. It's nothing personal.

ROXANNE: Nothing personal.

PIPPA: My book was right. Shoes are units. If I have the drive and determination, the desire and a dream, I can make it to the top.

ROXANNE: Dream ? Your little dream has no-- vision.

PIPPA: Vision? Vision is too expensive. It lowers the margin of profit. I brought some of your favorite scotch.

ROXANNE: Oh, thank God. *(she pulls two glasses out and slams them down amongst the shoes.)*

PIPPA: Let's celebrate. *(she raises her glass)* He's promoted me. *(Roxanne chokes on scotch)* Maximo is sending me to L.A. to supervise the West Coast operations, our move into both Arrow and P-Mart Stores.

ROXANNE: Congratulations.

PIPPA: You should save up, come out on vacation. Los Angeles is a footwear paradise. You'll never find a city with more pedicures. You'd love it.

ROXANNE: Thank you, but I prefer classic cities. I despise car culture. Outdoor pools.

PIPPA: Not even to see it?

ROXANNE: Pippa, darling. There are some things you don't need to see.^^^Do me a favor.

PIPPA: Of course.

ROXANNE: Hold a shoe. Channel its personality.

PIPPA: Which one?

ROXANNE: Any one.

PIPPA: ^^^I can't.

ROXANNE: Kick yourself off. Fake it. Try one of your own line.

PIPPA: ^^^ "Ohmigawd, I've got to get something good for the prom."^^^ Nothing.

ROXANNE: Nothing?

PIPPA: Nothing.

ROXANNE: How long have you known?

PIPPA: For some time. Roxanne, why can't I do it anymore?

ROXANNE: Don't worry about it dear. Simply one of the things you've lost along the way.

PIPPA: I've always been able to—get some feeling from the shoes—do you remember when we channeled the Art History Professor-Queen-Fleur de Lis together?

ROXANNE: You're right. We really had something. Together. Pippa, it's not too late. Don't you see? Don't sell these. Not here. Our clients--they'll all stay away.

PIPPA: It's just a corner of the boutique.

ROXANNE: It will taint everything.

PIPPA: I hope your personal feelings about this collection won't hamper you ability to sell it.

ROXANNE: Don't worry about me Pippa. I can sell your shoes faster than anybody. Faster than you. "Hilda, as a personal favour to me—will you buy some shoes for your maid?" I'll sell your shoes so well they will fly off the shelves. Fly. Off. The shelves. Tourists. Young girls. "Souvenir of the city? Yes, you could buy these at home, in P-Mart, but you'll always remember being at the flagship store, where it all began." We're done here Pippa. Congratulations. Don't you have to pack?

(Pippa exits.)

ROXANNE: *(She picks up a New Direction box, reads:)* "This new line is dedicated to and inspired by those on a limited income, a single mother who is trying to stretch her secretarial paycheck to feed three kids."—Good God. Don't worry about it. Don't worry about it. I'll inspire him again. I will. I will. I'm his muse. I inspire him to greatness. *(pacing the shop, nervously, composes herself for a final assault, dials her phone)* Bon journo, Maximo. We must speak. Yes, yes. They are...cute. But Momo, sit for a moment. I've been thinking about our mamas, yes, I have been. I loved your story, how she had bare feet but she would look at Life magazine left by the G.I.s and clip out the photographs of shoes. She pasted them on her wall, and dreamed. My mama was the same. In our mama's day, if you could afford it, you bought the best you could, chair, sofa, car. It endured. Think of the shoes Bacall, Gardner, Loren used to wear. Classic. Leave the knockoffs to someone else. Maximo, you have to have something to knock off, for God's sake. It would shock the fashion world if you stopped. Yes, take out a full page ad in the Times. In all the papers. A return to quality.

Numbers be damned. We owe it to our mothers. Yes, darling, they would be so proud of us, they would.

Scene Ten: Kneel

Six months later.

(Roxanne laying out a new collection with ecstasy, reading labels. Pippa enters.)

ROXANNE: Pippa. Darling. How ARE you?

PIPPA: You should know.

ROXANNE: Nothing personal sweetie.

PIPPA: Couldn't rest until you had me ousted, could you?

ROXANNE: All's fair in sales, darling. I had values to maintain.^^^ What are you doing now? ^^^Darling, you look so bleak.^^^ I could give you your old place back. .^^^ If you don't try anything strange.

PIPPA: And what? Be second to you? For always? ^^^^What's the new collection?

ROXANNE: A celebration of classic Hollywood. "Blue Angel." Dietrich on a swing, kicking up her heels.

PIPPA: Oh, how—old school.

ROXANNE: You've lost. Be gracious. Congratulate me.

PIPPA: Congratulations. You've won. You've got your shop back the way you like it. But Roxanne—

ROXANNE: What?

PIPPA: Roxanne, in some ways, I was just pretending to be what you wanted me to be…but I thought there was more to it. I thought when you got to know me…

ROXANNE: What are you here for?

PIPPA: Fit me.

ROXANNE: What?

PIPPA: Fit me. For a pair of shoes. I want to celebrate.

ROXANNE: Your severance package from Tremendulo? Darling, you might want to save that.

PIPPA: I would never celebrate a severance. Fit me.

ROXANNE: You've lost me. Did you come into some money? Win the lottery? Get lucky in Vegas?

PIPPA: P-Mart put me in charge of fashion acquisition. I make six figures.

ROXANNE: Excuse me?

PIPPA: I did it. I'm a client now. And, Roxie, I did it through sales. Sales. It wasn't marriage, it wasn't the lottery, I earned it. And I get credit for it. You're right about the shoes being quality, but you never saw what the idea of moving units, of tapping into desire, could do for you personally. And to top it off, I've written a book, me. *(hands Roxanne a copy)*

ROXANNE: *(reading title)* "More Than Units: Your Desire Will Make You Rich."

PIPPA: It'll be a best seller. I'll never have to kneel again. Bring out the champagne. Discern what I want. Pick out a pair for me.

ROXANNE: Certainly Mademoiselle.

PIPPA: So formal. Isn't it your job to be intimate with me?

ROXANNE: As you wish, Pippa. "Barefoot Contessa" uses the latest techniques to create a shoe that is nearly invisible—

PIPPA: You aren't listening. I don't want to be invisible.

ROXANNE: Darling, you're missing the point. They aren't about invisibility.

PIPPA: How dare you challenge me? Switch tactics.

ROXANNE: I thought you loved a challenge. These are about magic. Supporting an impossible arch through improbable means. Aerodynamics. Skill.

PIPPA: I hate them.

ROXANNE: Might I ask—are you thinking of a certain color?

(Roxanne is non-assertive in her approach. Pippa notices and approves.)

PIPPA: Pink. The color of success.

ROXANNE: I have just the thing.

PIPPA: ^^^^Aren't you going to bring me champagne?

ROXANNE: Of course. Congratulations. I always knew you'd be a success. I did. And look at you. You look fabulous. One moment. *(exits to get the champagne)*

(Pippa, alone with the shoes, she can't help but admire their delicate construction. Once again, she tries to get a feeling from the shoes, but fails. She throws herself onto the sofa.)

ROXANNE: *(Roxanne comes back, glass of champagne)* Since you're such an insider, I might be able to do something special. I could convince Tremendulo to fit you for some prototypes he is working on for next year. He's been inspired by his childhood in Italy, the color of the flowers, the wildness of horses running in a field, the comfort of his Mama's cooking—does that evoke anything for you?

PIPPA: My mother ran off.

ROXANNE: I'm terribly sorry.

PIPPA: Don't bullshit me. I know you don't care. Comfort me with the shoes, Roxanne. Comfort me with shoes.

(Roxanne kneels and tries shoes on Pippa. Pippa stretches out. She does not help Roxanne strap them on her feet in the least. She admires different pairs from the side. The exact opposite of the opening image of the play. Slow fade.)

<u>THE END</u>

AT WATER'S EDGE
by Elaine Avila

Recipient, Alden B. Dow Fellowship, Midland, Michigan

For Winona Avila

Characters:

Cecilia Thomas, 50s, Architect

Alice Abe-Flores, 30s, Client, Wife to Paul, Japanese-Canadian

Paulo Flores, 30s, Client, Husband to Alice, Portuguese-American

(In Act II, Alice plays the Ghost of Leopoldina, Paulo's Grandmother; and Paulo plays the Ghost of Philippe, Cecilia's deceased husband)

Setting: The house the characters dream of building. Various other locales: Cecilia's office, Alice's apartment, Paulo's work, a parking lot.

Note on Setting: *The house, designs, models might never be seen-- they can be suggested by light and the actors' imaginations.*

Premiere: Cor Departure Theatre at Performance Works, Vancouver, BC, Canada, 2005,

directed by Thrasso Petras
Paulo........Bob Frazer
Alice........Maiko Bae Yamamoto
Cynthia......Corrina Akeson

Showcase Readings, Canadian Center for Theatre Creation, with Harry Judge as Paulo, Tiffany Ayalik as Alice, Marianne Copithorne as Cynthia, directed by Kathleen Weiss, Greenwood Studios at Seattle Rep, with Andrew Litzsky as Paulo, Molly Lyons as Cynthia and Kathy Hsieh as Alice, directed by the author, Richmond Gateway Theatre, Scene First, with Paul Moniz de Sá as Paulo, Valerie Sing Turner as Alice, and Molly Lyons as Cynthia, directed by Barbara Tomasic

Special Thanks: Bill Clark, Suzan-Lori Parks; Kathleen Weiss, Molly Lyons, Ian Farthing, Simon Johnston, Barbara Tomasic, Richmond Gateway Theatre, Rachel Ditor, Dennis Smeal, Literary Manager, Arden Theater; Thrasso Petras, cor departure, Kathleen Weiss, Kim Tough, Brian Bauman, Sibyl O'Malley, Sigrid Gilmer, Heidi Carlson, Claire Fogel, Jamie Clark, Wilson Durward, Evergreen Cultural Centre, Daniel Lomas, Koerner Foundation, Vancouver Foundation, Hamber Foundation, Government of British Columbia, The Alden B. Dow Creativity Center; Dr. Grover Proctor; Liz Drake, Gail Bender; Daria Potts, Director, Alden B. Dow Archives; Alden B. Dow Home and Studio, Donald J. Koster (AIA), President, Dow-Howell-Gilmore Associates Inc; Dr. Mary-Margaret Munski (AIA), Cecili Williams, Hilario Saavadra, Kat Oschsner, Alexis Salas, Leo Hobaica, Terence McFarland, Celeste Den, Carla Nassy.

Bob Frazer as Paulo and Maiko Bae Yamamoto as Alice in the Cor Departure Production of At Water's Edge, Performance Works, Vancouver, BC, Canada, 2004 (Photo Courtesy of David Cooper/Cor Departure)

ACT ONE.

SCENE ONE.

THE OFFICE OF ARCHITECT, CECILIA THOMAS. VANCOUVER, B.C.

(The office is designed to set off Cecilia and her work: to highlight the sky, water and mountains; to be elegant, formal and intimidating to clients.)

CECILIA: Do you plan to have children?

ALICE *(simultaneous):* No.

PAULO *(simultaneous):* We haven't decided.

CECILIA: Will your parents come live with you as they age?

ALICE: My parents are no longer living.

CECILIA: I'm sorry.

PAULO: I don't want my parents in a facility.

ALICE: Can we talk about this later?

(Cecilia pulls out a pad and writes and sketches.)

CECILIA: Do you work at home? What are your hobbies? Who cooks? Who cleans?

PAULO: Why do you need to know who cooks?

CECILIA: Counter heights. Sink heights. I'll need your

heights. Is it a party kitchen, a re-heating of take out food space, or do you actually…cook?

PAULO: I cook. A minha Avó--my grandmother-- taught me.

ALICE: Counter heights? I never thought of any of this.

CECILIA: The specifics of your dream. Any hobbies?

ALICE: I don't have time.

PAULO: I play racquetball.

ALICE: What with saving to buy the land—

PAULO: I fish, hike—I need hobbies to socialize with clients.

CECILIA: *(makes a note)* Then, Mr. Flores, you'll need room to store rods, reels, athletic equipment.

PAULO: Call me Paul.

ALICE: It's Paulo. *(the 'o' is pronounced 'ooo'.)*

CECILIA: Paulooo. That's lovely.

ALICE: The Portuguese pronunciation.

CECILIA: Why do you change it?

PAULO: No-one speaks Portuguese.

CECILIA: What do you do Mrs. Abe-Flores?

ALICE: *(corrects her Portuguese pronunciation)* Flores.

CECILIA: Flores.

ALICE: Call me Alice, please. *(pause)* What do I do?

CECILIA: For a living?

ALICE: Oh, I see. Forgive me, I'm--*(gasping for breath)* I'm--

CECILIA: Are you all right? Can we go on? *(They nod)*

ALICE: Graphic design.

CECILIA: Ah, an artist. *(makes a note.)*

ALICE: I'm not an artist. More of a presenter. I do layout. Compared to you, I'm hardly an artist at all--

CECILIA: But you do have a visual nature. And you, Mr. Flores—

PAULO: I own my own business.

CECILIA: Ah. *(makes a note)* An entrepreneur.

PAULO: I'm in information management systems.

CECILIA: I'm always fascinated by people who make jobs where there were none before. You work at home?

ALICE: No.

PAULO: When you run your own company, you are

always at work. Everywhere is your office.

CECILIA: The world is your think tank.

ALICE: He has huge contracts—the Canadian government is planning to put all of our medical records online. That will be done by Paulo's company.

CECILIA: You're American?

PAULO: How can you tell?

CECILIA: Attitude. Hmm. You got a contract from the Canadian Government?

PAULO: I have the background, the experience. I gave the best quote.

CECILIA: I see. Your cultural backgrounds, how do they figure in?

ALICE: Figure in? I'm Canadian. I don't know the first thing about Japan.

CECILIA: The Japanese have had a huge influence on North American architecture.

ALICE: I prefer to leave the great weight of history out of it.

CECILIA: Fascinating. You believe you can create a building entirely new? Completely modern. No precedent.

ALICE: Don't you?

CECILIA: No. Paulo, what of your cultural background?

PAULO: Being Portuguese is, being of one of the 'folk'--sailors, workers, immigrants-- or being one of the rulers-colonizers, slave traders—I just work in computers.

ALICE: Exactly.

CECILIA: Curious.

PAULO: Alice and I, we can make a new life—

ALICE: Unburdened by history.

PAULO: That's what you do with each commission, isn't it?

ALICE: Create something new?

PAULO: That's never been seen?

CECILIA: We share that passion, yes. What do you own?

PAULO: *(overlapping)* A Lexus—

CECILIA: What do you plan to own? Furniture, clothes, books, art? Are the things you own flat like photographs and paintings or three dimensional like vases and sculptures?

ALICE: We haven't had time to collect…art.

PAULO: But we might.

ALICE: The house will be a work of art.

CECILIA: I'll need photographs of all of your possessions. I'll send someone 'round to do it. Don't clean up. I want to see how you really live.

PAULO: Why?

CECILIA: I can tell a great deal from a client's possessions.

ALICE: We live in a tiny apartment. When Paulo moved in, we put everything in boxes. We could unpack.

(Cecilia whips out a Polaroid camera, gestures for them to move together and takes a shot.)

CECILIA: Knowing both of you is as important as topography, as essential as engineering. Many forces inspire a building. Your things reveal a great deal about you. *(she examines the photo, smiles.)* Hmm. *(this makes Paulo and Alice very uncomfortable.)* Do you entertain at home? Another couple, or fifty? More? Paulo, how big will your parties be?

ALICE: Fifty people?!

CECILIA: It happens. Especially in a business like your husband's—
Forgive me. Some clients do have panic attacks during this type of meeting. Water?

(They shake their heads 'no,' clasp hands, breathe deeply.)

CECILIA (CON'T): It has something to do with the client considering his or her life. Now I show you some images and you tell me what your eyes are drawn to.

PAULO: I feel like I'm being psychoanalyzed!

CECILIA: This isn't about neurosis. It's about discovering what you love. Your first impressions. *(images fall across the back of the theatre, via slides/powerpoint/overhead projector)* What are you drawn to? What do you see?

Le Courbusier's Chapel in Ronchamp, View from the South.

PAULO: Sails, ships on the sea.

ALICE: The impossible made possible.

A Raven Mask, from the Northwest Coast.

PAULO: Aspiration, reaching out.

ALICE: Transformation.

Chrysler Building, New York City.

PAULO: Razzle-dazzle.

ALICE: Mr. Chrysler put a toilet on the top so he could pee on all his employees.

PAULO: I thought they said "shit."

ALICE: I was trying to be polite.

CECILIA: You are both right. Chrysler. What a client. *(she laughs)*

A tee-pee.

PAULO: Little babies, wrapped in fur, warm, swaddled.

ALICE: Dried meat. Beef jerky. Having to move.

An African Village.

PAULO: Community.

ALICE: Suffocating closeness.

A Chinese Pagoda.

PAULO: Birds.

ALICE: Concubines.

Frank Lloyd Wright's Robie House.

PAULO: Possibility.

ALICE: Beauty.

PAULO: Beauty.

ALICE: Love. Musical.

PAULO: Harmony.

Monet's Water Lilies

PAULO: Key chains, umbrellas, mouse pads.

ALICE: Monet was going blind when he painted those. They're elemental like notes, like paint, the beautiful sound of certain words, like Paulo's name. Paulo.

CECILIA: That's sweet.

ALICE: Like Beethoven composing when he was going deaf. Loving what you might lose.

CECILIA: *(shaken)* Hmmm. Thank you for the meeting.

ALICE: Did we pass? Will you design our home?

CECILIA: Designing a home is very intimate, very involved. I'll have to consider this carefully.

PAULO: When can we get you out to see the site?

ALICE: Yes. The land. It's amazing. On Gambier Island.

PAULO: You'll fall in love with it.

ALICE: The way the sea meets the sky meets the land, one becomes the other…

PAULO: The views of the straight…the mountains etched with snow gullies….

CECILIA: I'll have my assistant call you.

(They exit, elated. Cecilia flashes through more images, they affect her physically—whether they are straight or curved, upward reaching or outwardly expansive. She ends on Monet's Water Lilies, struck by the feelings of love and loss.)

SCENE TWO.

A DUMPSTER. VANCOUVER.

(Alice is about to throw a box into the garbage. Paulo enters, stops her.)

PAULO: Alice. Alice. She said, and I quote, "don't clean up."

ALICE: She didn't mean it. Ah!! Our place is full of junk!

PAULO: It's too small!

ALICE: If I had rented a bigger apartment, I couldn't have afforded to buy the land.

PAULO: *(discovering a stuffed animal in box)* Not Mr. Wiggles!

ALICE: It's tacky! Grimy!

PAULO: It's Mr. Wiggles!

ALICE: What do you need it for?

PAULO: I've been saving him... what if some kid wants to come over to play?

ALICE: We can't design our whole life around Mr. Wiggles!

PAULO: This is how we live. With odd things we happen to cherish.

ALICE: Dust collectors.

(Simultaneous. Cecilia enters finishing up a lecture at the University of British Columbia. She is not aware of Alice and Paulo and they are not aware of her.)

CECILIA: Interview the client. By all means. They feel

they have been heard. Use what they tell you. But only if it inspires you. Their needs must not dictate your design. What does the average person know about building? Are we to spend our lives creating, in essence, boxes for holding whatever junk our clients happen to have? Remember, ultimately, your design is a record of your beliefs about how to contain life itself. What do you, the architect, hold most sacred? These values should be in every millimeter of your design. Is it nature? Intimacy? Transparency? I'll tell you a secret. Most of the time, your clients have no idea what they want.

ALICE: When was the last time you looked at Mr. Wiggles?

PAULO: I like knowing he's there.

ALICE: Right. *(hands toy to Paulo)* Shall we ask for a special shrine to be built in the house for him? *(pause)* Paulo. What if she won't take us on?

PAULO: Okay. *(pause)* I'll hide him for now.

ALICE: Deal.

CECILIA: Work with me. You are making breakfast. That's it, stand up, pretend you are in your kitchen. You reach for the eggs. Where are they? Does the refrigerator door open on a side that faces your cooking area or away from it? Where is the pan? Way over there? You have to close the cabinet to open the dishwasher? The counter is too small for the dish drainer? My point is made. Thank you, you may sit down.

PAULO: Her questions were a bit—

ALICE: Invasive?

CECILIA: Most people live with abysmal design. Most people inherit something that doesn't work for them. They make the best of it, they accommodate themselves.

PAULO: I felt completely judged. *(imitating Cecilia)* "You're American?"

ALICE: She loved you! *(imitating Cecilia)* "You're an entrepreneur? I'm always fascinated by people who make jobs where there were none before."

PAULO: It was intense. Our whole lives, collapsed into this…quiz.

ALICE: I was beginning to panic.

CECILIA: This has created an erosion of aesthetic appreciation. Why are we destroying the natural environment? Because most people have to ignore their immediate surroundings, just to get through the day! Why do we no longer vote? Because we feel we cannot change even our apartments.

ALICE: The money…

PAULO: Money should be used.

ALICE: Can we afford it?

PAULO: I want to do this for you. Imagine living in a Cecilia Thomas home.

ALICE: I never thought I would.

CECILIA: Yes, yes, a residential commission can be a nightmare. I no longer have to do them. I choose to.

ALICE: She is so strong. She knows what she wants and goes after it.

PAULO: But a little…I don't know…something… sad.

ALICE: I wonder why?

PAULO: Is she married?

ALICE: I don't think so.

CECILIA: For next week, design an efficient kitchen. It's a challenge. You've probably never been in one.

(Cecilia turns off the projector and exits.)

ALICE: Did you know her father was an architect?

PAULO: No. Who was he?

ALICE: Justin Thomas. He designed half of downtown. In the sixties.

PAULO: Plain stuff.

ALICE Form equals function. He left wilderness out of the equation.

PAULO: Do you think he interviewed his clients the way she does?

ALICE: No.

PAULO: Maybe that's why she's sad. The weight of all of our stories.

ALICE: I didn't think she was sad. She seems fabulous.

PAULO: A bit of a front, don't you think?

ALICE: Imagine living in a place she made for us--God!

PAULO: It will happen Alice. It will happen….for us.

(His cell rings, he gestures, he's got to take the call, and exits. Alice continues throwing various dusty treasures into the dumpster. She tries to throw out Mr. Wiggles, he grabs the toy before she can.)

SCENE THREE.

CECILIA'S OFFICE

PAULO: All their belongings sold to pay for their own internment. Her grandparents lost everything. Packed off to build their own housing in huge snow drifts. Her uncle died. Even after the war, the government wouldn't let her family move back. They had to work on someone else's farm in the prairies. All of them in a one bedroom hovel. Cracks in the walls, freezing in the winter. Alice's parents never got their health back.

CECILIA: British Columbia. Such beauty. So many scars.

PAULO: When Alice was little, she'd make her own house out of old boxes. After her parents died, she used the restitution money to buy the land. Alice is the first person in her family to own property again.

CECILIA: Mr. Flores, I empathize—

PAULO: Isn't there anything I can say?

CECILIA: I'll be frank. You have a complete lack of consensus. That makes your project impossible.

PAULO: What does that mean?

CECILIA: What is your home for? To work? To rest? Both? You're not sure if you want room for children or parents. Is it to be a getaway for the two of you? A vacation home? Entertaining is more important to you than Alice-- In my experience—

PAULO: If we can get together on those points, you'll build our house?

CECILIA: I would try harder to fit you into my schedule. I can't promise.

PAULO: Tell me, what do you see? For me and Alice.

CECILIA: I have had a few thoughts.

PAULO: C'mon. What are they? I wish you would come out and see the land. It's one of the most beautiful places in all of Western Canada. We have amazing views of Howe Sound and the Straights of Georgia. Unless you find the design challenges of our project insurmountable—

CECILIA: There is not much that I find "insurmountable" Mr. Flores.

PAULO: Right. Of course not.

CECILIA: I have been mulling some ideas around…

PAULO: Go on.

CECILIA: You'll want to impress your clients. Large parties would be in order, showing off your spectacular setting, attracting major contracts…

PAULO: Exactly. Brilliant.

CECILIA: But I don't understand.

PAULO: What?

CECILIA: You don't want anything of Portugal, of your childhood in this house?

PAULO: Like what?

CECILIA: Do you own any family heirlooms?

PAULO: No. My family were peasants. I made a lot of money two years ago. But I haven't had time to buy…much.

CECILIA: Is there anything that makes you think "Portuguese"?

PAULO: No.

CECILIA: Anything your grandfather or grandmother gave you?

PAULO: After my grandmother died, my mother gave me a tablecloth...

CECILIA: A tablecloth.

PAULO: My grandmother came to America for an education she never got. Never saw her mother, or her sisters again.

CECILIA: Did she write to them?

PAULO: She signed her name with an X. But she'd make tablecloths. And mail them to her sisters, and they'd mail ones they made back.

CECILIA: How unusual. Probably meant more than a letter.

PAULO: She'd make such tiny stitches. She could have been a surgeon.

CECILIA: She and her sisters must have spent days and nights sewing together. Learning that art. Where do you keep that tablecloth now?

PAULO: I don't know. A box, a drawer.

CECILIA: I could build that tablecloth right into the design of the kitchen.

PAULO: The past. In my business we are always talking about the future.

CECILIA: Your ideas of home are rooted in your past.

PAULO: That's saudades...

CECILIA: What does that mean?

PAULO: The Portuguese look at the sea and yearn for what might have been. They call it saudades.

CECILIA: They? Not you?

PAULO: Here some people manage to keep their language, their culture. In America, they try to forget. My Dad became American. He hardly spoke Portuguese…I've tried to learn…but it's all…rubbed out. If I can get consensus with Alice will you build our house?

CECILIA: I'd have to see the site.

PAULO: Great, then you're coming.

SCENE FOUR.

A PARKING LOT.

PAULO: Bear with me. *(he holds up a piece of chalk.)* We are going to draw the house.

ALICE: Why?

PAULO: I met with her.

ALICE: Without me?

PAULO: She'll only do it if we can come to an agreement on what we want.

ALICE: We're in agreement.

PAULO: It boils down to three main points. One, are we going to have children?

ALICE: Paulo! I can't discuss that. In the middle of a parking lot.

PAULO: Two, are we going to take care of our aging parents? Three, what sort of entertaining will we do? We've got to give her some kind of consensus, so she can work with us.

ALICE: I don't see why we can't work these issues out AFTER we have the house.

PAULO: She believes that the design for the house must contain our lives now and our future. It's the brilliance of having something made, specifically for us. Please, Alice.

ALICE: Go ahead.

PAULO: This....*(he draws a square on the floor, Alice waits impatiently)*

ALICE: Is what?

PAULO: Is a room. A square room. What do you want it to be?

ALICE: It doesn't have any doors.

PAULO: Maybe it's the foyer.

ALICE: Why do we need a foyer?

PAULO: I don't know. Airflow. Breeze...space.

Somewhere to take off your shoes, put on your coat. You do it. You're the designer.

ALICE: I don't see how we can work out major issues in our relationship by drawing a floor plan in the middle of a parking lot! I'm not one of your employees. This isn't an issue we can solve with one of your exercises.

PAULO: What do you suggest?

ALICE: Let's build the house, then let life...unfold.

PAULO: Please. Make a mark on the pavement.

ALICE: I don't want to. I can't. I can't.

PAULO: Why not?

ALICE: Every mark might be a reason—

PAULO: For what?

ALICE: For you to leave me.

PAULO: Oh, Alice. I promised to never leave you. That's marriage. *(they embrace.)* Please. Draw.

ALICE: It's too flat here. I can't draw on concrete. Our house will be on uneven ground. We're not going to pour a foundation. We're going to build on stilts so it doesn't disturb the forest floor.

PAULO: That's great. That's a decision. Stilts! Draw!*(pause)* Alice, I'm not going all over town looking for bumpy concrete to give you perfect accuracy.*(drawing)* You'll want your own workroom, with lots of light.

ALICE: I don't need all that.

PAULO: What if you decide to paint? Make things of your own?

ALICE: *(incredibly moved)* Oh, Paulo.

PAULO: I'll take a basement office, how do you draw that?

ALICE: Paulo. We decided on stilts—there won't be any basement.

PAULO: I need dark. Then I can see my computer screens.

ALICE: That's what curtains are for.

PAULO: The living room. Entertaining. It's got to be big enough for parties for my job—

ALICE: Only if they are catered.

PAULO: I agree. You're a terrible cook.

ALICE: *(laughing, hits his arm)* Oh, Paulo.

PAULO: The bedrooms. Cecilia needs to know—should she build a room, a suite… for my parents to live with us—not now—when they get older. We can talk about it. We can.

ALICE: It's too isolated.

PAULO: Okay.

ALICE: I'm not a big caretaker. I did it for my parents. I don't think I could-- go through that again.

PAULO: Okay. Great. Children.

ALICE: Granddad always talked about this awful feeling...of not being able to protect his kids. Having children. It's not for me.

PAULO: Alice, we're not living in an internment camp.

ALICE: You don't...get it.

PAULO: I do.

ALICE: How could you? You have a family.

PAULO: Why is this only your decision?

ALICE: Why do you want me to have children?

PAULO: God. We're so close.

ALICE: It's you that won't agree.

PAULO: No kids. Okay. Okay. It's fine with me. It is. We're done. We can go see her. What's wrong?

ALICE: Are you sure? About your parents? About kids?

PAULO: Yes. It's fine.

ALICE: It's all so set.

PAULO: We can erase it, see?

ALICE: Not once it's built.

SCENE FIVE.

ENGLISH BAY.

PAULO: *(rehearsing a phone call to Cecilia)* No kids. No kids. There's no need to build a room. For a child. For children. We're a couple pursuing—into—our own fulfillment. We don't want to be tied down. We don't even want a dog. A goldfish. A plant. It'll be easier to go on vacation. We like our sleep. No. No room for my Mom and Dad. A guest room. Nothing permanent. *(he looks at the phone, is unable to make himself dial.)*

SCENE SIX.

LECTURE HALL. UNIVERSITY OF BRITISH COLUMBIA.

(Cecilia is teaching her class. Paulo sneaks in during her lecture.)

CECILIA: The history of great buildings is filled with sacrifice. Slaves constructed the world's most famous monuments. Workers on great bridges plummeted to their death. Kings went bankrupt, building their tombs. Frank Lloyd Wright forced his clients to subvert their entire lives-- possessions, life style, furniture, even their clothing...to match his design. What will you give up to achieve greatness? Ah. That's time. See you on Thursday. Paulo!

PAULO: Is that what you believe? We should subvert our lives to your design?

CECILIA: This class is for architects. Not clients.

PAULO: Who makes the sacrifice?

CECILIA: Everyone. Mr. Flores, I'm working to get these students to strengthen their dreams. Architects today are all about pleasing the client, pleasing the builder. Vision is rare.

PAULO: That's why they've brought you in to teach.

CECILIA: Yes. *(she gathers up her notes and papers, he helps).* I haven't had anyone help me with my books, since—for some time.

PAULO: Hard to believe.

CECILIA: What are you doing here?

PAULO: Learning.

CECILIA: Don't you have to work now?

PAULO: When I pursue something, I pursue it.

CECILIA: I see.

PAULO: I'm here to learn what you look for in a client. You like sacrifice.

CECILIA: Bravery, innovation, excitement. All these require sacrifice. My clients are pioneers, willing to invest in a better way of living.

PAULO: You value decisiveness.

CECILIA: How can you make a building if your clients don't know what it is for?

PAULO: We've made decisions. We have consensus. Why haven't you come to see the site? Your assistant is putting me off. Meet us in Horseshoe Bay at Noon. At the dock.*(he hands her the papers, they attempt to shake hands, laugh.)*

CECILIA: You're very persistent Mr. Flores. Until then.

SCENE SEVEN.

GAMBIER ISLAND. ALICE'S PROPERTY.

(Cecilia enters, paces over the topography of the land. As she exits, Alice and Paulo enter.)

ALICE: She's thorough.

PAULO: What's she doing?

ALICE: She's exploring the topography.

PAULO: She finds every rock, every cranny. She doesn't even write it down.

ALICE: She is memorizing it in her body.

PAULO: She's memorizing everything—-our site, our finances, our relationship, our domestic details. It's a little scary—

ALICE: But exhilarating.

(Alice smiles and nods. They kiss. Cecilia enters.)

CECILIA: It's as beautiful as you say.

ALICE: We're decisive. We'll have big parties. I'm not all that social. But marriage is—

PAULO: Giving up. Giving over.

CECILIA: I'm not looking for you to be my ideal clients, I want you to be yourselves.

PAULO: No problem. We can fake that. *(They all laugh)*

CECILIA: Alice. You bought land. Not a home. A dream for the future. Why this plot? Why an island?

ALICE: The real estate agent advised me to find one of those neighborhoods, you know, trashy now, junkies, prostitutes, boarded up, but with possibilities. Some artists fixing it up, rumors that property costs will quadruple, get in now. It made me sick. I felt I'd be taking land from these people who had so little. The agent suggested an island. When I saw the sparkling lights from the water through the trees-- see it? There-- I thought those little dots of light were spirits--people who died, now free, dancing--

CECILIA: Yes. The sunlight on the water seems to float towards us.

ALICE: I know island life has problems—

PAULO: Small town hoakiness—

ALICE: Having to plan groceries so far ahead—-racing to the ferry, risking feeling trapped. But this spot said "yes."

I didn't know what I'd build—I couldn't afford much—a shack—a retirement place—sometimes I'd camp out here—but then I met Paulo.

PAULO: She had this book, it was about your buildings—

ALICE: I've always loved your work.

PAULO: When I saw Alice's land, your book…

ALICE: He put it together.

CECILIA: If I design your house, I'd like to capture some part of the happy moments of your marriage.

PAULO: Were you married?

CECILIA: Once. It didn't last. What are your best moments…together? Times you wish… would never move forward…or would slow down to a near stop. Never be forgotten.

ALICE: Mine is Tofino. You shouldn't have spent so much money on me.

PAULO: Wasn't it worth it?

ALICE: The wind from across the ocean… smashing the wood and water and seaweed into the long, long sand… then.. that cozy fireplace.

PAULO: Whew. Can you capture that in a house?

ALICE: Artists like Cecilia push the boundaries of what everyone thinks is "possible." Paulo, what's your moment?

PAULO: It'll seem silly--

ALICE: What?

PAULO: The way you made me a logo-- you put an image to paper for my company. Then you put it on our website, and it glowed from within. It was like watching a wish appear. *(sees the look on Cecilia's face)* What? Shall I show you around?

CECILIA: By all means.

PAULO: That tree, embracing the other tree is my favorite.

ALICE: And the cedars--sheltering this little cove, teeming with all this lovely sea life, hoping not to smash anything as you walk around, knowing you are the steward of this place—

CECILIA: Can't help squashing some life—

ALICE: But dreading that crunching sound—wanting to keep it pristine.

CECILIA: This place is incredible.

PAULO: Will you do it?

ALICE: Please?

CECILIA: Yes. I'll do it.

ALICE: Ohmigaaaaawd!!!

(Paulo pulls out a bottle of champagne and three glasses.)

CECILIA: How did you know I'd say yes?

PAULO: I had a feeling.

ALICE: Oh, Paulo.

(She embraces him. Cecilia looks on and smiles, wistfully.)

SCENE EIGHT.

CECILIA'S OFFICE.

(She is drawing, erasing, re-drawing. She flashes a topographical map of the land on her slide projector, runs her hands across the image on the screen.)

CECILIA: *(quoting Paulo)* "Being Portuguese is being one of the folk, sailors"...

(She flips on her slide projector, slides of shells, sea life, Portugal, Portuguese sailing boats, flash across the screen. She responds physically.)

CECILIA: "Logo, making a wish appear..."

(She flashes pictures of Japan on the screen, their fishing culture.)

CECILIA: *(quoting Alice)* "The way the sky meets the sea meets the land, one becomes the other..."

(She goes to the models, spins it, dissatisfied, tries again, pulls back a wall—gets a big idea—)

CECILIA: Teeming with life…

(She flashes back across the images of sea life, moves her body in the shape of a shell, feeling the curve.)

SCENE NINE.

CECILIA'S OFFICE.

CECILIA; Ready? *(she unrolls a large sketch on the table)* It's a starfish, with stilts placing half of the house over the sea! Here boats can dock. Here, in the main room, the glass floors make it possible to watch the tides come in and out. These arms or wings on the forest side can be offices or guest rooms—

PAULO: Wow. It's fantastic!

CECILIA: Alice?

ALICE: *(pause)* Why… a starfish?

CECILIA: It's an astounding form of life. What is a starfish but an animal that bridges the gap between land and sea? This is the very virtue of your property.

ALICE: Oh.

CECILIA: It's a radial design, working from the outside in and the inside out. Like a mandala. A labyrinth.

PAULO: Alice. Isn't there anything you like about it?

ALICE: *(pause)* It's on stilts.

CECILIA: Yes. The way to work in a forest is to perch above it, to let it be. Pouring a concrete foundation. It's a cheat. It levels what's there.

ALICE: *(pause)* I'm sure it will... enhance your career. People will write about it.

CECILIA: What seems to be the problem?

ALICE: I'm not a part of it. Not a part of it at all.

CECILIA: Your remarks about protecting sea life--

ALICE: It's a showplace.

CECILIA: If you don't see yourself reflected here, you might attempt to answer the many questions I put to you.

ALICE: I have.

CECILIA: Mrs. Abe-Flores, I suggest, since you are an artist—Why not make a design yourself?

ALICE: Design it myself.

CECILIA: Alice can draw. Maybe that would be the best way for her to contribute.

ALICE: No.

PAULO: Alice, this is your dream.

CECILIA: Let me. When Paulo explained that your grandparents were interned...that your parents were unable to recover financially...

ALICE: Paulo what?

CECILIA: He was very convincing. He said you used to design houses out of old boxes--

ALICE: That was personal.

CECILIA: Alice, why can't he tell me something about you--

ALICE: That is not something about me. It is a historical fact about this country.

PAULO: Alice, I was trying to get her to design the house—

ALICE: And this is how you go about it?

CECILIA: Why do you care that he told me?

ALICE: It's terrible. This country wanted to erase my family. Paulo. I never told you that you could discuss—-

PAULO: God. Alice. You wanted me to get her onboard.

ALICE: Is that why you're working with us? Good god.

CECILIA: That's what intimacy is, Alice—people knowing each other.

ALICE: What do you know about it? You're divorced.

CECILIA: I'm not divorced.

ALICE: You said you were married.

CECILIA: I was.

ALICE: Where is he then?

CECILIA: He died.

ALICE: Oh. Oh my god. I'm sorry. I didn't mean to—

CECILIA: It's okay. I don't mind if you know. Cancer. We were in our twenties. But I married him anyway.

PAULO: You knew when you married him? Why did you do it?

CECILIA: I hoped he'd—live. Philippe was very determined. He gave me many gifts. Standing up to my father—

PAULO: The architect?

CECILIA: Yes. When my Dad was building in the sixties, they had all these funny features to the buildings-- little foyers and hallways and boxy rooms. I wanted openness, to echo the beauty we see around us, not conquer it. Philippe gave me the courage to break through. Dad hated my work after that. But I didn't care. It takes courage to do this. To stand together. Alice, do some drawings, get yourself to manifest your dream on paper. Then we can try again.

SCENE TEN.

ALICE'S CRAMPED APARTMENT.

(Alice is working with a pad and paper, crossing out, re-drawing, frustrated.)

PAULO: What's wrong with it?

ALICE: I can't get it to open out! To start small on the forest side, then to spread out like the ocean. If I put workrooms for us on the third floor, see, on the ocean side-- do you see?

PAULO: What is that? A sink?

ALICE: No. It's your computer room. You can close the drapes by remote control.

PAULO: Great.

ALICE: I thought you'd like that. But if I put the workrooms and our bedrooms against the sea, it blocks the light on the lower floors. It's all lines, squares, circles, I can't seem to--I'm just moving boxes around.

PAULO: Isn't that what architecture is?

ALICE: No!

PAULO: Why don't you find floor plans you like and take the parts that work for you—

ALICE: No.

PAULO: Treat it like a computer program. We take prototypes, patterns that have worked before and re-assemble them to perform specific tasks.

ALICE: No. Paulo. It's got to be original.

(Alice crosses to the fireplace, about to throw the drawings into the fire.)

PAULO: Alice, stop it.

ALICE: Paulo. Let me BURN them.

PAULO: No. You've worked so hard on these.

ALICE: All the more reason to be free of them—

PAULO: Alice, stop it.

ALICE: Where will I be? Where? I'd thought I'd have something, not easily erased. Something.

PAULO: Oh, Alice, you can't be erased. Let's go back to her. Show her what you've done. I'll make it happen for us. I promise.

SCENE ELEVEN.

CECILIA'S OFFICE.

ALICE: Seeing the dark lines of your sketch against that bright white paper--it was a shock. Every line is a decision. My drawings—I'm so frustrated.

CECILIA: Frustration is fine. It always leads somewhere. Somewhere else.

PAULO: Her drawings are terrific.

CECILIA: Let's see them.

ALICE: I was looking for a place to burn them—

CECILIA: *(looking at drawings)* My, Alice. Ever thought of working as a draftswoman?

ALICE: No.

CECILIA: These are very good. Technically, I mean. Ah, you couldn't get it to open out.*(Alice nods)* Alice, why do you want my work to surround you for a lifetime?

ALICE: Something in me falls away when I go into your buildings. A feeling I had when I was young. The wallpaper in this house we rented was yellowing and curling, and there was this awful stain... spreading and spreading. I hated the winter, hated the rain, because it forced me inside, watching that terrible stain. You probably don't understand. You and Paulo, the house where you grew up, your parents owned it. It was in the background, supporting you. My grandparents lost everything, their home, their business, things that had been in our family for generations—their china, their kimono, their Buddhist shrine...The Government sold all of their belongings to pay for their internment. My family had to start over with nothing. Less than nothing, they'd lost their health. I watched my parents...*(she trails off, it's too painful to finish)* That's what falls away, when I step into one of your buildings.

CECILIA: What were your grandparents dreaming of when they moved here? Tell me something good from your family. Something pure. Something no-one can take.

ALICE: I can't. It's been... erased.

PAULO: Oh Alice.

ALICE: We've all been assimilated.

CECILIA: Alice. There must be something.

(Alice starts to cry.)

ALICE: There's not.

CECILIA: Let's simplify. Easier questions. What do you want to see? First thing? When you wake up? Trees? Sky? Dark drapes? The shimmer of water?

ALICE: Trees.

CECILIA: Paulo?

PAULO: Sky.

CECILIA: Open. Open out. *(she takes a piece of cardboard from the starfish model, takes a simple model of a house glues part of the undulating wall from the starfish onto it, gets Alice to hold a corner, then pulls off part of the roof)* Have it open—*(she bends the roof back)* open out—in your bedroom you'll wake and see—

ALICE: *(joking)* Rain? Tears?

CECILIA: The subtleties of clouds. *(she begins flashing images of glass)* I see…natural light—…

ALICE: See how the light filters through—that's what we want.

CECILIA: Low emissivity glass. Very good for the environment.

PAULO: God. It's beautiful.

ALICE: What? The glass?

PAULO: To see you passionate about it. Articulate. Saying what you want.

CECILIA: At last. I'm finally getting a read on you. Also, *(she pulls out polaroids)* these are useless. My assistant said not to clean up. I want to know how you really live. I'll come out tomorrow.

SCENE TWELVE.

LECTURE HALL.

CECILIA: To make a building, to work with a client, always involves some sort of compromise-- yes, yes, I realize this is a change from what I said earlier. But we change. Sometimes our clients affect…us. A building is a coming together of many, many forces. Your clients are facing certain truths about themselves, truths that are made manifest in the walls you construct for them. I want you to profile a friend, family member, associate. Create a house for them, while staying true to your ideals.

SCENE THIRTEEN.

SNAPSHOTS. CECILIA'S OFFICE.

(Cecilia is looking at a transparency of the ground plan of Alice and Paulo's apartment via overhead projector. She draws Alice and Paulo's trajectories as they speak, on the ground plan, with a marker.)

(Alice and Paulo, moving through their apartment, on separate trajectories.)

ALICE: We wake up, see the grey sky, hear the seagulls cry, hear the rumble of the elevator in the building, the distant slam of doors, hear the whirr of car tires spitting out water on pavement—

PAULO: My cellphone starts ringing at 6am, and stops at midnight. I advise on whatever crisis—

ALICE: I drink a coffee—

PAULO: I race back and forth trying to get a professional look together—

ALICE & PAULO: We collide into each other—

ALICE: Sorry.

PAULO: Sorry.

ALICE: Excuse me.

PAULO: It's cramped.

ALICE: Small.

PAULO: I run into the edges of the walls.

ALICE: And I'm gone. I grab breakfast on the way to work—We both work late, grab dinner out.

PAULO: I go in, not much room to work at home.

CECILIA: City dwellers. Moving to an island. Telecommuting. You'll use your new home in a new way. You're moving into your ideal life.

> *(Pause, Paulo nods. They exit. Cecilia sketches, pulls out her model, works on it, covers it with a cloth.)*

SCENE FOURTEEN.

CECILIA'S OFFICE.

> *(Alice and Paulo looking nervously at a red silk cloth covering a model of their house.)*

CECILIA: My inspiration was you—the building is an ongoing conversation between Paulo and Alice, Forest and Sea. I call it "At Water's Edge." Paulo, because of your devotion to Alice—at times I see you as the forest, supporting life—at others, as the ocean, opening up Alice's world. Alice, sometimes you're like a forest, with your intricacies, then like an ocean with your yearning—*(she pulls the cloth up so they can see it, but the audience cannot)* Voila! It undulates because of the topography of the forest floor. Each side has elements of the other. On the ocean side it's very open, but it has organic forms arching out of the beams—

ALICE: Like trees.

CECILIA: The piece de résistance is this glass wall. Here it tapers off and curves like a wave. We'll sprinkle ground glass throughout the wall. When the light hits it a certain way, it will glint, as the ocean does in sunshine.

PAULO: It's musical.

CECILIA: Ah, yes, thank you, I want areas of your home to have different acoustics—here sound is absorbed, here it will echo... This wall is inspired by the intricate stitches in your grandmother's tablecloth, these shapes in the glass—look closely, an echo—

ALICE: *(tears make her eyes shine)* Of a kimono. A Buddhist shrine. China patterns.

CECILIA: Then you approve?

ALICE: Oh, yes.

PAULO: More than you know.

CECILIA: Can I phone the contractor?

PAULO: Yes.

ALICE: May I?

(Cecilia nods. Alice crouches down to be closer to the model, which is still unseen by the audience. Paulo watches Alice. She is radiant.)

PAULO: *(to Cecilia)* You've done it.

(Cecilia nods and smiles.)

INTERMISSION

ACT TWO

SCENE ONE.

THE SITE.

(Cecilia is being interviewed by a television crew about the house)

CECILIA: What is extraordinary about this project is that the husband and the wife are strong in their distinct natures. This is also a feature of their property. The forest and the sea are distinct. Rather than mishmash everything together, I've celebrated this separateness.

(Paulo and Alice are touring the foundations. Paulo touches a beam.)

ALICE: That wood improves with wear.

PAULO: You don't want wood to wear, you want it to resist wear.

ALICE: What?

PAULO: Chipping, warping, moisture. Bugs. You don't want that to happen. You resist. You sand, you stain, you shellac.

ALICE: It improves.

PAULO: Because Cecilia said so?

ALICE: Weren't you listening? Because cherry reddens in the sunlight, it—

PAULO: Honey, it rains all the time.

ALICE: Not all the time.

PAULO: I give. How does the wood improve with wear?

ALICE: *(a come on)* Shall I show you?

PAULO: Alice!

ALICE: Do you improve with a little wear?

PAULO: Alice. You're making it impossible—I can't resist you.

ALICE: Don't. Don't resist me. *(they kiss, she comes up for air)* I feel different, don't you?

PAULO: Different how?

ALICE: The house. It makes me feel grander-- do you feel that Paulo? That you could be anything? Doesn't being here make you feel you could do something amazing? It will surround us, it feels like it loves us. I've never been so fulfilled.

PAULO: You haven't been fulfilled?

ALICE: I used to see people getting excited when they saw each other, smiling, laughing, going to dinner, shopping for clothes. It felt like a lot of noise. Alot of money going out.

PAULO: Alice, with me you didn't worry about noise. You could forget about money, right?

ALICE: Sometimes.

PAULO: People running, laughing, smiling, being together…when you're with me…you're one of them, right?

ALICE: Yes. Now I feel a part of everything. A little scared.

PAULO: Of what?

ALICE: When I was little, my sisters ran and screamed and played, I'd go in the back and stack my boxes, building us a home. Cut windows and doors, rip flaps to fit into other flaps so I could stack them higher and higher. Then the rains came and reduced it all to a sodden mess. It made me fear things... collapsing. Take off your helmet. C'mon. Nothing is going to fall on us. There's no roof. There. *(she ruffles his hair)* Let me give you a tour. Here is your nook by the fire where I'll curl around you... *(she kisses him.)* Here is where you will work--all this space, an easy chair, an ocean view, and I'll bring you coffee and kiss you and distract you from your work—

PAULO: Distract me. Distract me. *(he buries his face in her hair, kisses her neck.)* Let's make a baby. Wouldn't it be magical? On the first time we made love in our new home, open to the sky, like a cathedral—

ALICE: Paulo, what, did you think the house would suddenly change my mind?

PAULO: Don't you wonder what it would feel like to do it? Here, in the foundations of our new home, open to the forest, the sky? Open to possibility? Unobstructed. In every way. Don't you want to?

ALICE: Paulo, it takes a month of not taking birth control pills for me to be "unobstructed."

PAULO: Don't be so practical. Let's pretend. Let's see how it would feel. It's what our bodies want to do.

CECILIA: I'll capture the way the couple combines their histories, legacies, to make a new future.

(The camera lights turn off.)

CECILIA: Go, go, get your shots of the property. I'll be right there.

(Cecilia is alone. She looks up, around.)

CECILIA: Philippe. I'm here. I'm still here. I can feel you, in the skin and bones of this house.

(She runs out after the crew.)

SCENE TWO.

(Later, that night. Paulo and Alice in sleeping bags on the land. Alice can't sleep. She tries to call to the ghost of her grandpa. His ghost never arrives.)

ALICE: Nono. Grandpa. I've forgotten your face. Nono,—Can I trust the land, the home will be mine, year after year? Would a baby be safe? When I was I child, I didn't know. The pain of missing you would last my whole life.

(Alice falls asleep. Paulo's dream. Alice becomes Leopoldina, Paulo's grandmother. She is stitching a tablecloth.)

PAULO: Avó! *(he kneels next to her as she works, leans his head against her.)* Does it help?

LEOPOLDINA: Working always helps Paulo. When you work, you feel less sad.

PAULO: I work.

LEOPOLDINA: You are a good boy Paulo. Why so sad?

PAULO: My wife, Alice, she doesn't know if she wants children.

LEOPOLDINA: What sort of a wife is that?

PAULO: She's not sure if she wants to take care of my parents.

LEOPOLDINA: What does she think marriage is for?

PAULO: Times have changed Avó, we can choose what it is for.

LEOPOLDINA: Santa Caterina of the crazy people. Do you go to church?

PAULO: No—

LEOPOLDINA: How do you keep the village together?

PAULO: I don't know, Avó.

LEOPOLDINA: The way you are living is crazy Paulo. I don't know why you come to me, this is not what we did in our life. I married, I was a good wife, I raised my children. What did you marry for?

PAULO: Love. I love her.

LEOPOLDINA: Paulo, you could go out behind a barn for that. You don't need to take a wife.

PAULO: *(referring to tablecloth)* Who are you making this for? Your sister?

LEOPOLDINA: It is for you. For your family. It isn't to put under glass. It is to mess up-- over family meals, to clean to mess up to clean to mess, again and again, to use.

PAULO: Muito obrigado Avó.

LEOPOLDINA: De nada. You're a good boy, Paulo. A Good boy.

(Leopoldina exits. Paulo stares up at the sky.)

SCENE THREE

ALICE AND PAULOS' APARTMENT.

(Alice enters with Paulo's suits under her arm. He is working on his computer.)

ALICE: Paulo—

PAULO: What?

ALICE: You're always working.

PAULO: I need every minute.

ALICE: Is there something I can do?

PAULO: Nothing.

ALICE: Have you eaten?

(Paulo waves in the direction of the garbage)

ALICE: Take-out?

PAULO: Alice, what did you think I'd have to do? To afford our life, I have to work. Hard. My grandparents were peasants, fisherman. Just like yours. Honey, we're nouveau riche. We gotta work. Thanks for picking up my suits.

ALICE: Do you need anything?

PAULO: Like what?

ALICE: I never imagined it would be like this.

PAULO: Is that an apology?

ALICE: Paulo, I'm not sure who I am anymore. If I'd never met you, I'd just be going along, carefully saving. I would have done something simple, an A frame, a cabin...but you made me believe—

PAULO: I didn't make you believe anything.

ALICE: You made me believe the house could be everything, everything I ever wanted--my favorite architect --do you think it's been easy for me? I never see you. You encouraged me to say what I wanted and now it's happening and you're always busy.

PAULO: What do you want?

ALICE: Come out to the house with me on Sunday.

PAULO: I have to work.

ALICE: Let me show you how it's grown. Please.

PAULO: Stop pushing me.

SCENE FOUR

LECTURE HALL. UNIVERSITY OF BRITISH COLUMBIA.

CECILIA: This house is a testament to modern marriage. No longer confined to roles, each member of a marriage can define themselves. Each element of the house is equally strong, equally distinct. We enter the house via a dark stone passageway, compressing space, heightening mystery. The foyer has a low ceiling, so we are led through the entranceway, discouraged from lingering. Then we open upon a sweeping panorama. We are led into my radial design. Round and round, each view more spectacular than the last. This is like all journeys, unknown, obscure, mysterious, a space you have to move through before you reach clarity.

SCENE FIVE

THE SITE.

ALICE: *(on her cell)* I'm handling it Paulo. *(hangs up)*

CECILIA: *(entering)* Handling what?

ALICE: Paulo's worried about the wood.

CECILIA: Here? It's cherry. It improves with wear. Sunlight makes it more red.

ALICE: Paulo wants it treated. He's worried about bugs.

CECILIA: You won't get bugs.

ALICE: I know.

CECILIA: This isn't about treating the wood, is it?

ALICE: What do you mean?

CECILIA: Is he happy with the house?

ALICE: He's very enthusiastic.

CECILIA: Where is he?

ALICE: Working. I love it. It makes me feel I could do anything—

CECILIA: But?

ALICE: But what?

CECILIA: You called the meeting.

ALICE: I'm pregnant.

CECILIA: What? I mean, congratulations.

ALICE: I haven't told Paulo. I have to find the right moment. But I have to tell you—the house—it will affect the design.

CECILIA: It certainly will.

ALICE: Take my studio. Change it into a nursery. It's not what you think—I wanted to be an artist, when I was younger. It's not for me. It's so much more than a job. It takes your soul.

CECILIA: There is too much light in the studio for it to function as a nursery. This entire project is far from child proof.

ALICE: I know.

CECILIA: The studio is far from your bedroom—a long way to go, even with child monitors.

ALICE: Please.

CECILIA: I don't know Alice. I put you through the lengthy interview process to avoid—you don't have any more big changes coming, do you?

ALICE: Oh, no. No, no, no.

(Alice's phone rings. She exits. Cecilia looks up.)

CECILIA: These people.

(Dream Sequence. Paulo enters, as Philippe.)

PHILIPPE: This isn't for me.

CECILIA: Philippe?

PHILIPPE: I hate it.

CECILIA: Why?

PHILIPPE: I didn't want a tribute. I wanted to live.

CECILIA: This is for us.

PHILIPPE: We would have never made this. We lived in different times.

CECILIA: You made me feel like a forest, mysterious, even to myself. You were the ocean, making my world stretch out in all directions.

PHILIPPE: You're missing who they are. They're full of secrets.

CECILIA: Stay. I want to remember this curve in your shoulder, the shape of your cheek—

PHILIPPE: I wasn't perfect. That's the worst part of dying. When people idealize you. They're getting the chance we never did…to change…

CECILIA: Stay, stay.

PHILIPPE: You know I don't belong here.

CECILIA: I'm eleven. Wearing a hard hat in Daddy's building—the walls are going up, up, up, covering the steel beams and everywhere the tap tap tap of hammers. Daddy is showing me all around. He never thinks a girl, me, will ever be able to do all this. I see he is sad I'm not a boy. I'm sad I'm not a boy. Daddy's walls go up covering skies and trees and views. I start to cry and

Philippe comes and takes me by the hand. He takes me round and round the maze of the building, leading me out, showing me the slender threads within me that can lead me to make something else. Philippe tears down the walls, something I would never dare. Outside can move inside. Philippe is gone and I must do it alone, alone. Alone.

SCENE SEVEN

LATER. THE SITE.

(Paulo pacing. Cecilia enters.)

PAULO: Have you ever agreed to something, made decisions… It's like water is all over me, above me. I can't break through. I thought I could live out here. It means so much to Alice. But it's too remote—all this water—what about storms? Getting cut off. What if my parents get sick? What if we change our minds and want kids?

CECILIA: You tell me this now?

PAULO: When am I supposed to tell you?

CECILIA: Maybe when I interviewed you. Maybe before we broke ground? Maybe before we hired the carpenters and built half the house? Any of those moments would have been good. But now?

PAULO: I can't keep silent any longer.

CECILIA: Mr. Flores, I know you want to make this happen no matter what. But you're throwing this project into chaos.

PAULO: What do you suggest?

CECILIA: Talk to your wife.

PAULO: I can't.

CECILIA: You told me.

PAULO: I thought I could handle these decisions—her decisions. But I can't.

CECILIA: Mr. Flores. I can't speak to you until you speak to your wife. I can't keep building this house until you work this out. This is becoming absurd.

PAULO: How long do you think I've got? Before I have to tell her?

CECILIA: I think you should tell her now.

PAULO: I've got to find the right moment—

CECILIA: There won't be one.

SCENE EIGHT.

THE SITE.

> *(Lights change. The sound of the ocean. Alice enters, admiring the house, touching details. Paulo follows her.)*

ALICE: It is incredible. We made this. Our love made this. Look at my wall. It's opalescent, different in each sort of light—gray, blue green--See how it glistens?

PAULO: Like the water.

ALICE: I feel so alive here. Look at what we've done.

PAULO: Right. *(pause)* Alice. I can't live here.

ALICE: What?

PAULO: It's too… isolated.

ALICE: You bring this up now?

PAULO: I know. I tried. I spoke to Cecilia.

ALICE: You spoke with her? And not me?

PAULO: I was afraid.

ALICE: What are you saying?

PAULO: We could… sell the land—

ALICE: Sell my land.

PAULO: Alice, I'm asking for your help.

ALICE: Why did you keep this from me?

PAULO: I wanted to be strong. To give you the house like a magical present.

ALICE: When you see the house, finished, you'll forget all this. You will.

PAULO: No. I won't.

ALICE: Paulo, It's going to be beautiful. Amazing. Inspiring. Made out of our love.

PAULO: I thought I could take it. You not wanting to have kids, or take care of my parents, but it feels like you're rejecting a part of me. The part of me that moves into the future.

ALICE: How is abandoning our house going to help?

PAULO: I don't know. I love you. I'll try anything.

ALICE: Won't it kill you? Not to finish it?

PAULO: No. Finishing it… is killing me. *(he starts to smash, rip apart the house, lets out a scream of frustration)*

ALICE: What are you doing? Paulo. It's a work of art.

PAULO: IT'S EVERYTHING THAT STANDS BETWEEN US. Alice, we were so close, those late nights in Tofino, sheltered from the wind and the rain, huddled, whispering secrets, interested in every thought, inside each other, it didn't get any closer. Now, we have this fucking glass wall.

ALICE: It's a work of art. It will stand long after we die. What in your life has ever promised you that? Something enduring? Beyond death.

PAULO: Being with you.

ALICE: The house will bring us together. That's what art does.

PAULO: My grandmother's tablecloth brought her closer to her sister. That's art. Not this house. This isn't art.

ALICE: What is it then?

PAULO: I don't know. A tomb. A monument. We were going to make a new future, remember? Fuck the past.

ALICE: Paulo, you're panicking. Let's go to sleep. Rest. When you wake up tomorrow it will all make sense.

PAULO: What if it doesn't?

ALICE: It's what I've done for years. Get up, work, keep the world turning. That's what people do.

PAULO: I think it all began with Mr. Wiggles. At the dumpster. That's when we started hiding who we are. I wish we could go back six months, a year, replay everything and see if it would come out differently. Alice, it's our last chance. Come with me. Forget about this place. Let's leave. Right now.

ALICE: You're talking crazy.

PAULO: No. I'm not. Come with me now.

ALICE: Or what?

PAULO: If you don't leave with me now, I'll know you never loved me.

ALICE: I love you.

PAULO: You only care for this house.

ALICE: This is for you! For us. Look at it.

PAULO: All I see is how our love failed, how you wanted the house more than me.

ALICE: No, Paulo. No.

PAULO: You can keep the house. I..I'll give it to you. *(exits)*

ALICE: No. Paulo. Paulo. That magical day in our new home, the house open to the sky like a cathedral… our baby entered through the margin of error…slipping past statistics…98% effective, 96% chance, our baby, already an exception. My body is a house, a home, a sea for a little transparent creature. Oh, Paulo.

SCENE NINE.

THE HOUSE.

(Cecilia rushes in, carrying a bottle of champagne and three glasses. Alice is very still.)

CECILIA: Sorry I'm late--

ALICE: The house. It's perfect. I love touching it. It's like a seashell.

CECILIA: I'm happy with the walkways. On the forest side.

ALICE: When I look up, I feel as if I'm swept up in the spiral of the trees, floating, not bound to earth.

CECILIA: And the playroom. I put all my love of

childhood into that room.

ALICE: I feel it.

CECILIA: Thank you. You're such a dear. Where's Paulo? I want to pop this open. *(she does, it spills out, Cecilia pours a glass, offers it to Alice, who takes it. Cecilia pours another)* Have a sip. I'm sure a sip won't hurt the baby.

ALICE: *(Alice sets the glass down, without drinking.)* He had to... leave.

CECILIA: What? Is he coming back?

ALICE: I don't think so.

CECILIA: Oh. Did you tell him about the baby?

ALICE: I was afraid.

CECILIA: He seems to love you so much.

ALICE: He does.

CECILIA: Has he left... for good?

(Alice nods, tears in her eyes.)

ALICE: He said...he'd give me the house.

(Cecilia stares at her glass of champagne. She can't drink it.)

ALICE: Don't be sad. It's perfect, perfect.

CECILIA: The house-- won't it remind you of Paulo?

ALICE: I want it to remind me. That's why it's perfect, a happier time, caught in amber.

(Cecilia is sad and stunned. Alice looks up, entranced by the house.)

CECILIA: I feel terrible.

ALICE: How can you say that?

CECILIA: Making decisions for your whole life. Setting them here. In glass. Wood. Copper. Stone. This house drove you apart.

ALICE: This house is the most perfect thing I've ever had in my life. It makes me feel safe. Every minute that I spend in this house will be a revelation. It's perfect, perfect.

THE END

Burn Gloom
Rituals on Millennium Eve
by Elaine Avila

Recipient, Canada Council Millennium Grant

Burn Gloom was created with Reports on What Happened Around the World on Millennium Eve, December 31, 1999 (9pm) to January 1, 2000 (1am) from : Christopher Mooney, Belle-Ile, France; Michael Vonn, Vancouver, British Columbia; Linda Mancini, Montreal, Quebec.; Shaun Phillips, Malawi, Africa; Colleen Lanki, Bali, Indonesia; Trina Eby, Singapore; Peter Hammond, Tasmania, Australia; Elaine Avila, New York City, U.S.A.; Alan Creighton-Kelly, Santiago, Chile; Trevor Found, Toronto, Ontario; Pat Rix, Sydney, Australia; Hu Fun, Ghangzhou, China

The Belle-Ile sections are co-written with Christopher Mooney.

The premiere of Burn Gloom *features original music by the Talking Pictures Ensemble: Ron Samworth, guitar; Peggy Lee, cello; Dylan van der Schyff, drums; Bill Clark, trumpet*

Special Thanks: Kathleen Weiss, Peter Anderson, Shaun Phillips, Maiko Yamamoto, Suzie Payne; Jessica Chambers, Mitchell Kezin, Heidi Specht, Ying Wong, Carmen Aguirre, Julia Varley, Laurie Brazzill, Carolyn Coulson-Grigsby, Alison Esposito, Bryon Grigsby, Bill Clark.

Premiere: Theatre Anima at Lab 1067, Vancouver, BC, Canada, 2001
Directed by Kathleen Weiss

Margaret............Suzie Payne
John.................Sean Phillips
Bridget..............Maiko Bae Yamamoto
Siobhan..............Elaine Avila

Suzie Payne as Emma in Burn Gloom *at Lab 1067, directed by Kathleen Weiss (Photo: Tim Matheson)*

Time: December 31, 1999--January 1, 2000

Music: *The jump cuts between scenes allow for musical compositions and improvisations.*

Characters:
There are four actors, who play four main characters. These actors also playing supporting roles in each others' stories.

AFRICA
Margaret, 50, Coca-Cola Executive

FRANCE
John, 38, Writer, Business Manuals

SINGAPORE
Bridget, 29, Choreographer

NEW YORK CITY
Siobhan, 34, Police Officer

Supporting Characters:

AFRICA
Lucy, Margaret's Daughter, 17
Falagimundala, African Elder, Malawi Village, 89
Florence, African Elder, Malawi Village, 90
Edes, Malawi Villager, 16

Ricky, Malawi Villager, 18
Toronto Party
John, Millionaire, Computer Software, 35
Suzanne, Aspiring Screenwriter, 33

FRANCE
Jillie, John's Wife, Freelance Translator, 32
Emma, John's Ex-Wife, British Nuclear Scientist, 40
Jean, a man who has lived his entire life on Belle-Ile, 78

SINGAPORE
Vancouver
Tristan, 37
Lorraine, 28
Montreal
Grandmother, 90

NEW YORK
Mike, Police Officer, 30
Tourist Mother
Tourist Daughter
Teenager 1
Teenager 2
Zena, the Psychic, ageless

AROUND THE WORLD
Zhang, Journalist, Ghangzhou, China, 28
Bob, Teenager, Tasmania, 17
Dorotea, Teacher, Chile, 40

Prologue:

    (Music: There is an overture, featuring musical themes from throughout the evening.)

Scene One: NEW YORK CITY

    (Siobhan enters. Standing on her beat, Times Square. Mike, another cop, enters with a styrofoam coffee cup. Music: Funk Groove with trumpet solo)

MIKE: Hey.

SIOBHAN: Hey Mike. Got your game face on?

MIKE: Oh, yeah.

SIOBHAN: 'Cuz, you know you can handle anything--

MIKE: --when you got your game face on.

    (Pause, they scan the crowd.)

MIKE (CON'T): What time do you have?

SIOBHAN: One minute to six.

MIKE: Fuck it's early.

SIOBHAN: Rough night?

MIKE: I wish. I haven't had a date in months.

SIOBHAN: Oh really? Me either. I wish men weren't such scum sucking pricks, you know what I'm saying?

MIKE: It's probably all that undercover prostitute stuff you do. What's your latest name?

SIOBHAN: Kitty.

MIKE: I like your real name. Siobhan. That's pretty.

SIOBHAN: It's Irish. I'd just like a guy to open the fucking door for me once in a while, you know what I'm saying?

MIKE: *(uncomfortable pause)* I'm going to get another coffee. You want one? *(she nods, he starts to exit)*

SIOBHAN: Yeah, sure.

TOURIST MOTHER: Excuse me, Officer, is this Times Square?

MIKE: Yeah. You're standing on it. *(he exits)*

TOURIST MOTHER: Really. It looks like a triangle. *(to daughter)* Honey, doesn't it look like a triangle?

TOURIST DAUGHTER: It's a lady. A lady cop.

TOURIST MOTHER: Well, I'll be! I just came for the ball drop, but, well, I'll be.

TOURIST DAUGHTER: Mom, this is so great. I've always wanted to have New Year's on Times Square...and I've always wanted my picture taken with a real New York cop. Are you a real New York cop?

SIOBHAN: Yeah.

TOURIST MOTHER: *(to daughter)* Are you sure you want a picture with a lady cop?

TOURIST DAUGHTER: *(awed)* Oh, wow. That would be so cool.

TOURIST MOTHER: *(to Siobhan)* That okay with you, ma'am? Should I call you ma'am?

SIOBHAN: Yeah. Sure. Whatever.

(They take a picture. Tourist Daughter tentatively shakes Siobhan's hand.)

TOURIST MOTHER: Officer, is it okay if we set up here? I want to be in the middle of EVERYTHING.

SIOBHAN: You got any alcohol?

TOURIST MOTHER: Uh, no officer.

SIOBHAN: Then it's okay.

(They use their scarves to stake out territory.)

TOURIST MOTHER: Where is the giant Coke sign? *(Siobhan points stage left.)* Oh, wow. It's giant, eh, sweetie? Where's the Lion King? *(Siobhan points stage right.)* Is it near the Disney Store? *(she nods).*

TOURIST DAUGHTER: Where's the MTV building? *(Siobhan continues pointing stage right.)* Cool!

(Cop's Nightmare 1: Music, Actor, and Choreography work with images of distant fear--for example, people screaming on the horizon. Siobhan is terrified--she does extreme physical movement in response to imaginary emergencies. The tourists move only slightly in response to the cop's movement— they are in another world.)

(Mike re-enters, with two coffees, breaking her nightmare.)

MIKE: Siobhan?

SIOBHAN: Guiliani is nuts. He should have listened to the Chief of Police. There is no way to secure this place…billboards, roof tops, man holes, windows…two million people.

MIKE: Did you hear about the noxious gas?

SIOBHAN: Yeah. Did you hear anything else?

MIKE: The word is it might go off at midnight, be prepared.

SIOBHAN: We still don't have gas masks…

MIKE: I know. "Be prepared." Right. Say your prayers, more like.

> *(The two tourist actors, roll over and become nonchalant·New York Teens.)*

TEEN 1: My mom? She's totally insane. She has all these cans of stuff in piles in the basement, gallons of bottled water, and mace. She keeps practicing with the mace 'cuz she's afraid somebody will take our food. I told her, "Mom! The mace is going to run out!"

TEEN 2: My mom is going home to Korea, she's going to go shopping at midnight.

TEEN 1: My Mom, she has all these piles of cans for each of us, all over the basement. But I humor her, I go, "um mom, I don't like that type of canned food," and she totally freaks out, "ohmigawd, honey, we'll put it in your sister's pile…what would you like instead? Corn?" She's totally nuts. She bought wood. I don't know what the wood is for.

TEEN 2: Y2K. No power. My Dad has fifty batteries. He tested twenty-seven flashlights last night. He made us pull our money out of the bank.

SIOBHAN: What is that?

MIKE: A giant whale puppet.

SIOBHAN: Oh.

Scene Two: AFRICA

(The Board Room scenes emerge out of a somewhat kitchy Africa window. Margaret writes on the walls of the set and on the African mannikin with chalk.)

MARGARET: Did you know Coca-Cola is the most recognized logo on the planet? 94% of humanity recognizes this great red and white swish! Did you know that we've been in Cuba and Panamá since 1906? By 1917, three million cokes sold per day, worldwide. Today, Coca-Cola products are served more than 705 million times everyday in more than 195 countries in every climate. *(to audience)* Care for a coke? Might as well. They're free. Help yourself.

Welcome to Zimbabwe. Look at this view. I can tell you its the nicest board room I've ever been in. Shall we settle down to business? I want to talk about our new trade package in Southern Africa and how you can be a part of it.

In twenty years, Africa's population will be greater than China's. The time is ripe for Coca-Cola to invest. Coca-Cola's presence in Africa will lead to economic growth and poverty reduction. More trade, less aid.

We are going to double African consumption of Coca-Cola in the next five years. This is where you come in. We want to you to be a part of our "Kusile" program…thats Nguru for "New Dawn." The year 2000 can be the most exciting and prosperous you've ever had.

Are you wondering why we flew you here? One: you can train and empower Africans to start their own businesses. Two: you can invest in Coca-Cola stock, enabling us to give Africans start-up capital. Oh, and three: you can just keep drinking our delicious beverage. Did you want a coke? Does anyone?

We want Africans to start up their own small businesses--ice plants, bottle washing factories, kiosk operators. And believe me, they do. The people here are amazing.

Scene Three: SINGAPORE

(Music: in Transition. Bridget's Theme. Guitar with clamps on the strings, Asian influences. Please Note: The phone calls in <u>Burn Gloom</u> work well when staged in a slightly abstract manner--actors might look at each other, circle around each other, move as if in their own environment, whether it's their apartment, the street, or a party. Real cell phones can be used. Tristan's rings. He pirouettes to pick it up. Lorraine is frozen upstage, like a manikin Tristan and Bridget look at her when they talk about her.)

TRISTAN: Hello?

BRIDGET: Tristan, is that you?

TRISTAN: Bridget. Oh, hi honey. Happy New Year's Eve.

BRIDGET: It's so good to hear your voice.

TRISTAN: Are you a real geisha yet? Are you back from Japan? Back in stifling Singapore?

BRIDGET: Yes, for Millennium Madness. Have a good one, by the way.

TRISTAN: Oh, how can I, honey? My plans have been ruined!

BRIDGET: I'm surprised to get you--I thought you'd be doing something more London-Paris-Rome-ish.

TRISTAN: Nope. I'm in dreary, drippy Vancouver. Constable Anne just got on the telly and said, "don't even think of going downtown."

BRIDGET: Almost as bad as Singapore! Our benevolent Dictator is hosting a non-alcoholic street party, complete with a lip-synching Ricky Martin impersonator.

TRISTAN: Is he cute?

BRIDGET: Oh, shut up.

TRISTAN: What are you doing tonight?

BRIDGET: Underground Lesbian Party.

TRISTAN: Why underground?

BRIDGET: I told you, its illegal to be gay here. You could get arrested, beaten with a cane, the whole bit. No-one is "out" over here.

TRISTAN: That's just ducky. I'm going to a dinner party. It should be swank, but if its not, I'll just DIE. I'm thinking of clubbing. *(pronounced "clooobing")*

BRIDGET: Like every other night. Have you seen Lorraine?

TRISTAN: I should be asking you that.

BRIDGET: C'mon, just tell me.

TRISTAN: I saw her at a party. She looks miserable. She's thinking of getting a dog. You should make nice. Really.

BRIDGET: I have to pay off my student loans, spread my wings. She understands.

TRISTAN: Don't be such a slut. She misses you. Phone her.

BRIDGET: Okay, okay! Its sounds like tonight could be bloody awful. It's the Millennium. It's too much pressure. Have you got your cell?

TRISTAN: Duh. Yes. I bought my own. My Ex went through cell phones like he went through underwear. And not mine.

BRIDGET: Let's make a pact to phone each other every few hours for company, to see if we're surviving, okay?

TRISTAN: I LOVE it! You clever girl. Talk to you in a few hours.

BRIDGET: 'K. Bye.

Scene Four: FRANCE

(Music: Interlude, Cello. Actors enter lugubriously with dining room chairs and sit on them wistfully. This has the effect of being comic—"ah! the tragedy of a bad party!" These scenes are played in a kind of suspended naturalism. The actors are hyperaware of one another. The actors exit, except for Jill. She re-arranges the chairs. John enters.)

JILL: Well! At least you're back in time for New Year's Eve dinner. Where were you and Emma all afternoon?

JOHN: The Mayor of Belle-Ile's Millennium Party. On the beach. You said you didn't mind watching the baby.

JILL: When I agreed to rent this house for the Millennium, I didn't think we'd be trapped here with your ex-wife.

JOHN: Is the storm my fault? Is it my fault that no-one could get here? That they stopped the ferries?

JILL: Of course not, John. I feel weird--especially with the baby--since you and Emma --

JOHN: I told you. Emma and I mutually decided not to get pregnant.

JILL: I feel uncomfortable.

JOHN: What can I do about it now? Jillie, lay off.

EMMA: *(entering)* Jill, I wish you could have come! It was great--it felt great-- like we were doing something. Not just sitting around, getting drunk, stuffing our faces. Which we were, too, of course, at the end--champagne, and galette des rois, cake of the Kings--donated by the Mayor. It was marvelous.

JILL: What was so great about it, exactly?

EMMA: We made a human chain stretching from the water's edge at the far end, across the beach, all the way up to the tops of the bluffs. John looked just smashing in his tuxedo, but he was wearing his ridiculous fucking rubber boots--

JOHN: What about you Emma? Rubber boots look just as silly with a ball gown.

EMMA: Waddling around like fucking ducks.

JOHN: So there Emma and I were, drinking champagne out of plastic cups. After we'd had our champagne and toasted the New Year and cursed the sons of bitches and everyone had driven away to get cleaned up, ready for their parties, there were these fucking plastic cups lying around on the beach, just tossed onto the bluffs.

EMMA: The wind from the storms blew them into every crevice.

(There is an uncomfortable pause.)

JILL: I got the goose. Eighteen pounds. And the oysters. They really are the best in the world.

JOHN: *(kisses Jill)* That's great Emma. *(He has confused their names.)*

JILL: Jill.

JOHN: *(uncomfortably)* Champagne for everyone?

EMMA: Yes, please.

JOHN: *(pouring)* Ah, bubbles bubble. The Millennium. I've been calculating my age tonight for thirty years.

EMMA: Me too! What a coincidence. I wonder why. It's so arbitrary, really.

(Silence.)

EMMA: Shall we watch the telly then? Before dinner.

JOHN: Emma!

EMMA: What is it now, John?

JOHN: All the miles.

EMMA: What?

JOHN: All that effort to be as far away from it all as possible and then to watch sad satellite-driven reports of it all. No TV tonight.

EMMA: Oh. well. I thought it might be…fun. Especially since…our dinner party has become a bit…abbreviated.

Interlude: STORIES FROM AROUND THE WORLD, Montreal

(These interludes allow for experimentation between actor and solo musician. We used guitar, with Italian/Nino Rota inspired music)

GRANDMA: I can't go out tonight.
It's too cold tonight.
I'm too old tonight.

But that's all right.

When I think of how poor we were in 1916 when we first arrived in Montreal from Italy and how cold it was.

We hardly had enough coal for the fire to keep us warm.

But not tonight.

Tonight I'm sitting in my kitchen a few hours before the clock strikes twelve.

I'm wearing my warm woolen socks.

My feet are warm tonight.

I still make all my clothes and food from scratch.

I have a big garden and I spend all autumn preserving foods for the winter.

The only time I go out in the winter is to go downtown to those internet cafes to see how the computers work, how they can hook you up to the rest of the world.

I think they're great.

Especially tonight.

I can't talk to you too long because my cough is getting worse.

But I'm so happy tonight.

The world is warm tonight. *(Adapted from a poem submitted by Linda Mancini)*

Scene Five: AFRICA

MARGARET: Let me tell you about the eager, hardworking youth I've met in Africa. We estimate that over 75% of the population is under thirty and available to work. On New Year's Eve, I had an experience that will illustrate just how eager they are.

If you're like me, you've never had a problem travelling that you couldn't solve with your American Express Card. Well, you haven't been in Africa, my friends. I borrowed a company land rover over New Year's. We were going to climb Mount Kilimanjaro for the Millennium, we signed up for a group tour to the top. Then my daughter Lucy decided she's be happier at home in Toronto. I started driving to Tanzania by myself.

Tiny little bolt from under the land rover comes loose.
Ratty youth hostel
 Lake Malawi, full up,
nowhere to stay
Monkey pees on my luggage.

(Three actors enter, singing traditional African songs. Movement structure, indicative of working in the fields.)

Chickens
Mango trees
Fields of Maize
   (Actors sing a different African song,
    a child's hand clapping game.)
Young woman invites me to her village,
where I can stay.
 (Actors surround Margaret, and laughing, pull her offstage.)

Scene Six: SINGAPORE

(Bridget is at her lesbian underground party in Singapore, talking to Manikins. Everyone she calls on the phone is real, everyone at the party is a manikin)

BRIDGET: When did I first know I was gay? C'mon you can do better than that! Some pick up line. All right, how about "when I first saw you, beautiful you."
What's your New Year's resolution? To have lots of sex? Ha,ha. And you? To go skinny dipping. To make more money. To smoke more. Oh, me? Me. Huh. I resolve to--I don't know. Practice more. Yes, I'm a dancer. A choreographer. I specialize in Japanese dance. You're a flaming lesbian? Great. You resolve to drink more? Me too. You're glad you're going to be dead for the next Millennium? Me, too, honey! Excuse me, I've got to make a phone call. *(she moves away. Music ends. Silence)* Lorraine?

LORRAINE: Bridget? Oh my god.

BRIDGET: Happy Millennium.

LORRAINE: Where are you now?

BRIDGET: Singapore.

LORRAINE: How was Japan? You must be dancing like a full fledged Geisha by now.

BRIDGET: Not quite! Some girls here--I mean women--they call each other girls at this party--they want me to do one of the dances.

LORRAINE: I'm sure it will be...beautiful. I have to go.

BRIDGET: Where?

LORRAINE: I'm going to walk the labyrinth at St. Paul's. I'd stay and talk, but I'm meeting someone.

BRIDGET: A new girlfriend?

LORRAINE: As if you have the right to ask. *(pause)* No.

BRIDGET: Do you miss me?

LORRAINE: Don't make me cry.

BRIDGET: I'm still in love with you.

LORRAINE: I--- I have to go. I'll be late.

BRIDGET: Can I call you later? I mean tonight. Everyone at this party is so plastic.

LORRAINE: Oh, Bridget, you're always exaggerating. Yes, you can call me later.

Scene Seven: FRANCE

(John, Emma, stretching after dinner.)

JOHN: I meet Parisians every day who look at me puzzled and say: "You left Canada?" -- It's true. "You left Canada? they say. "To live in France? *(Pause.)* Mais, pourquoi?"

EMMA: This is so not true.

JOHN: It is. All the time. The French think of Canada --

EMMA: Here we go.

JOHN: The French think of Canada… as some sort of vast expanse of pure promise --They all want to move there. All of them. Just to escape themselves, their limitations, the confines of their lives, the little cultural-historical holes they live in, that have been carved out for them by their revolution and their collaboration and their colonial arrogance and their crap pop music and their absurd poseur intellectuals and their shite films and their 365 different fucking cheeses. All of which they're also rather proud of, rather smug about. *(Jill enters.)* Oh, there you are. How's our Connor?

JILL: Asleep.

JOHN: Here's your one well deserved drink.

EMMA: How did you decide to have him?

JOHN: The baby? We lied to ourselves, we lied to each other, we stopped using birth control…and voila!

JILL: Emma, I hope you're not disappointed that you're not in Vancouver for New Year's. You have so many friends there.

EMMA: Ugh! Absurd place. Far too much spandex. Cuts off the circulation to the brain --

JOHN: You remember Jillie. It was Vancouver that broke us up. Emma couldn't stand the rain.

EMMA: It wasn't the rain.

JILL: What was it then? I mean, why didn't you like Vancouver?

EMMA: Unhealthy obsession with the bagel. Insidious preoccupation with menus and ingredients. Over-obsequious waiters who spend more time describing a dish than it takes to prepare or eat. Ridiculous men with bandannas on their head, using dogs as pick-up devices. All wearing the same designer glasses, Carrying the same lattés. Wearing the same aromatherapeutical colognes. *(in unison with John, who has been mumbling along, he knows this rant by heart)* Beach volleyball! So what made you choose Belle-Ile for New Year's, Jill?

JILL: John has been trying to plan this for over ten years--

JOHN: She knows.

JILL: We considered Argentina, the Outer Hebrides, but when we came here last summer--

JOHN: We decided right then and there...just a few close friends, good food, good wine, long walks on the beach, maybe a fire on the shore, roast a lamb on the spit, slurp back a few oysters--

EMMA: Sing some sea shanties--

JOHN: Then …

JILL: At midnight....

JOHN: As the rest of the world elsewhere goes loudly insane, we'd quietly face the ocean and raise our glasses to friends and families over there...in the New World....and the New Millennium. It would have been perfect. If it weren't for this fucking storm.

(Both Jill and Emma sigh. Jean, a man who has lived in Belle-Ile his entire life, enters.)

JEAN: Alo, Alo, do you have some wine for moi? For Jean?

JOHN: Hey, Jean! Entree, entree!

JILL: *(pulling him aside):* Are you sure this is a good idea?

JOHN: Oh I love old hairy Jean. *(sotto voce)* I invited him. Here you are.. *(he pours him a glass)*

(Jean drains it, and keeps getting John to fill his glass as much as possible during the scene. The three of them treat Jean like a pet or exotic animal)

EMMA: What have you got there?

JEAN: *(pulling a bird out from somewhere unusual)* C'est un guillemot. *(pronounced "gheelmoh")*

EMMA: What the fuck is a guillemot?

JILL: Guillemot are those very pretty black birds with white winged patches and bright red legs and feet. They are all over the island.

JOHN: Tasty, eh, Jean?

EMMA: Is that your dinner? I suppose the locals eat them.

JEAN: Je'sui bellilois moi, un vrai. *(drains glass, gets John to fill it)* Where are you from?

JOHN & JILL: Canada.

EMMA: I'm from England.

JEAN: Hmm.

JILL: You know Canada, Jean?

JEAN: No. *(long pause)* I've heard of it.

JOHN: You travel much, Jean?

JEAN: I've been to the continent.

ALL: Which one?

JEAN: *(puzzled):* Le continent *(points)* Quiberon. Une foi. Quand j'avit dix ans.

EMMA: You mean to tell me, you've lived here fifty years and only set foot off of Belle-Ile once?

JILL: And that was only to Quiberon, on the mainland, 45 minutes away?

JOHN: Here's to Jean, the real islander. Un vrais bellollois!

(They all raise their glasses).

ALL: THE REAL ISLANDER!!

Scene Eight: NEW YORK CITY

SIOBHAN: *(running onstage)* What is that? A fire?! *(She yells at a mannikin)*
WHAT THE HELL DO YOU THINK YOU'RE DOING? You can't have a fire in here! Jesus! Put that out! Listen, if you give me any more problems, you are out of this barricade, do you understand me? You can't

see anything from four or five blocks away, which is where you'll be. Got it? *(She recovers, then goes into her second nightmare--this one based on images of people jostling and crushing her, wearing "2000" glasses. Music: high affected, discordant long tones, fight choreography. Siobhan shakes off the nightmare. Mike enters.)* Even if we manage to catch every asshole with a gun, every idiot with a bomb....all it takes is somebody who wants to make a name for himself to kill us all.

MIKE: Same as every New Year's. Same as every day. What's with you?

SIOBHAN: Hear about the moron with the shotgun?

MIKE: Nope.

SIOBHAN: We got him. I've just been thinking.... some jerk today lights up a firecracker, everyone panics. Where do they look for help?

MIKE: Us.

SIOBHAN: They panic, they run, we get crushed to death.

MIKE: *(he takes her arms and holds them, looks deep into her eyes)* You're a good cop.

(Siobhan looks at Mike, startled, then crosses back to her "post.")

ZENA, THE PSYCHIC: *(thick Brooklyn accent or bizarrely exotic accent)* Hey you, Cop!

SIOBHAN: What seems to be the problem, ma'am?

ZENA: No problem. I am psychic. I have unique capabilities. I sense that you are someone who needs a break.

SIOBHAN: I've never been to a psychic.

ZENA: Relax. You'll be fine. Do you want the complete crystal ball reading, which includes your past, present and future, that's fifty dollars.

SIOBHAN: On a cop's salary?

ZENA: Or the palm reading, which covers who you are and points to directions in your future, that's twenty five dollars. Or the tarot card, just a general sense of what will happen, that's ten dollars.

SIOBHAN: *(considers a moment)* The tarot reading.

ZENA: *(obviously disappointed, she begins shuffling cards so worn that they are unrecognizable)* Fine.

SIOBHAN: I notice you're boarded up. *(laughs nervously)* Do you know something the rest of us don't? About terrorists? And New Year's?

ZENA: People are worried, very worried. Especially when they see me boarding my place up. But there's nothing to worry about. I'm just remodeling. Nothing will happen this year. But you should worry about next year...its the APOCOLYPSE. *(laying out cards)* You're a very sincere person. An honest person. A person who goes out of the way to right an injustice. How am I doing so far?

SIOBHAN: *(trying not to reveal much)* Are you sure? Is there anything about terrorists, violence?

ZENA: No, no, I see dark haired man, but this is romance. Maybe someone you work with....the attraction is dangerous because you might lose him as a friend, but it is also thrilling--

SIOBHAN: Yeah.

ZENA: You will be very lucky in 2000. After clearing up problems for common citizens, you will be recognized for your dedication to your work. *(finishes reading)* So, you're a cop. Do you have a minute?

SIOBHAN: Not really.

ZENA: My husband, he got a parking ticket yesterday, it was very unfair, he was in this store for two extra minutes longer than he meant to be, and then, this ticket. I thought you could help us out.

SIOBHAN: I have to go. Back to work.

ZENA: *(sarcastic)* Happy New Year!

(Siobhan crosses back to her post. She sees Mike from across the square and they eye each other slowly as they cross, a la Romeo and Juliet.)

Interlude: STORIES FROM AROUND THE WORLD
CHILE
(For Actor and Solo Trumpet)

DOROTEA: My night begins atop Cerro San Cristobal, the highest point in Santiago and home to La Virgen, the giant statue of the Virgin Mary. *(she lights a candle)* Many people converge here for dinner--everyone is out--from newborns to great great grandparents. No one gets babysat, no-one is left out and the night has no limits. The summer evening is warm, soft, calm--just how Chileans are described--Suavecitos. At midnight--lots of tears-- we hug and kiss all those that are close to us. I feel the vibrations from the fireworks outside and inside my body. Police watch, even laugh with pedestrians but touch no one, a very special night, a very different Chile from the seventeen years of the Dictatorship.

Scene Nine: FRANCE

(Jill scribbles onto a little piece of paper and then burns it in an ashtray. If fire paper is used, it can be thrown into the air. John rushes in, frightened.)

JOHN: Jesus! Jill! What are you doing!

JILL: Burning gloom.

JOHN: What is that?
      (Emma enters.)

JILL: It's a Spanish Tradition. From New Mexico. I read about it. *(She is entranced by where the fire has been.)*

EMMA: Jill! You never cease to surprise me. Whatever are you doing?

JOHN: It's some Martha Stewart thing. Its called "Burning Gloom."

EMMA: Burning Gloom? What is it exactly?

JILL: You write your one biggest regret from the past year on a piece of paper and burn it.

JOHN: Just one regret? I could write a book!

EMMA: Can I do it too?

JILL: Sure. *(she rises)* I'm going to bed. I'm exhausted, and I want to cuddle with the baby. You'll all have to countdown without me.

(Emma considers, writes a regret on a slip of fire paper, and lights it on fire.)

EMMA: Happy 21st Century, Jill.

JOHN: Good night, Jilllie. *(They kiss. Jill exits.)*

EMMA: She has much more spirit than you've led me to believe. *(he doesn't react)* Jo----hn....we've...had dinner.

JOHN: I know. The wreckage of two days cooking are waiting to be cleaned in the kitchen.

EMMA: We've seen the fireworks atop the Citadel--

JOHN: Such as they were. In the gusting winds.

EMMA: Let's watch the telly.

JOHN: Like any other night.

EMMA: I can't believe you're still such a snob.

JOHN: It's just that I haven't got any analytic hold on this event...the Millennium.
(Emma grabs the remote, we hear some television sounds.) Fine.

(SFX: Sound of channel surfing. New Year's Eve Television.)

EMMA: We've made it so far without anything blowing up.

JOHN: These boxes-- television, computers, internet...they make us feel connected, but we're not.

EMMA: What an insight. You never did learn to relax.

JOHN: *(rushes to window, or where window would be, downstage)* Lightening!

EMMA: It's not lightening, it's the flashover of high tension wires touching, then snapping apart, in the force of the wind. John, you are such a snob. Give me the remote back! Look it's "The Birds." They're about to destroy the human race. You can always count on Hitchcock.

> *(Lights flicker and out. Music: Storm. Actors (John, Jill, Emma) face front, in blankets.*
> *They are holding emergency candles or flashlights. Music: Storm-- building to a crescendo.*
> *The actors watch the storm at the "window," speechless. Music: Provides transition back to the*
> *Singapore Party, where Bridget is performing one of the dances of the Geisha (or part of a dance).*
> *She is not in full regalia, but probably wearing a kimono and a wig or upswept hair with a*
> *hair ornament. Lorraine, frozen, like manikin, upstage right, about to enter the labyrinth.*
> *Bridget uses Lorraine as a distant image of love in her performance.)*

Scene Ten: SINGAPORE

BRIDGET: *(She ends her performance and begins talking to manikins.)* Thank you! Yes, that was a dance based on my studies with the Geisha. . Actually, no, they aren't prostitutes. Geisha actually means "artist," they are highly refined professional entertainers. Excuse me, I have to make a call. Tristan?!

TRISTAN: Bridget? At last. I'm on Robson Street. Its hilarious! The stores hired all these temporary security guards, just for New Year's. I don't know what they are afraid of, the hockey riots were, what, hello, seven years ago? There is this one guy, in a turban, I think he is trying to disarm me with his smile. The dinner was fabulous, but I ended up at a community dance. There was crepe paper on the walls. I wanted to kill myself!

BRIDGET: I want to marry her.

TRISTAN: What? Who? *(brings his phone down, continues talking normally)*

BRIDGET: Lorraine. I want to marry Lorraine. *(brings her phone down.)*

TRISTAN: You're drunk.

BRIDGET: Not really.

TRISTAN: You just want her spousal benefits.

BRIDGET: No, I love her.

TRISTAN: Oh, sweetie. Well, then! Do it. You can do it.

(Music Piece. Lorraine begins walking in a large arc.)

LORRAINE: In the labyrinth, you lose track of time. As much as the path doubles back on itself, there are no blind ends in a labyrinth. It's all part of the way out. Or the way in. One foot in front of the other.

Scene Eleven: AFRICA

(Music: Acapella African song. Edes, a young girl, sits with her head bowed, and translates for Faligimundala. Although the actor speaks English in the play, the convention reveals cultural difference and provides opportunity for comedy.)

MARGARET: I sat with two of the village elders, just watching the fireflies. They reminded me of my grandparents back in their village in Wales....I asked one elder- he has forty grandchildren and five wives, imagine- Does the year 2000 mean anything to you?

EDES/TRANSLATOR: Does the year 2000 mean anything to you?

FALAGIMUNDALA: Nothing.

EDES/TRANSLATOR: He says, "nothing."

MARGARET: He must have seen many changes in his life...

FALAGIMUNDALA: *(everything he says is carefully considered)* In those days the crops used to have a high yield, but now the soil has lost its fertility.
In those days money had a value, but nowadays it is valueless.

EDES/TRANSLATOR: He says the crops are bad.

FALGIMUNDALA: In those days, people used to eat together. They were all meeting at Agogo's house--

MARGARET: Agogo?

FALAGIMUNDALA: *(recognizing that Margaret is using an African or Chichewa word)* Eh, ah.

EDES/TRANSLATOR: Grandfather.

FALAGIMUNDALA: But nowadays, each house is alone.

EDES/ TRANSLATOR: Each house is alone.

FLORENCE: *(siting at edge of mat, one of Falagimundala's wives)* It seems as though God has taken care of me the whole time and to me, reaching 2000 is a great achievement.

MARGARET: Your English is good!

FLORENCE: I don't know what it will bring. I am in suspense. But it is a praise to God that I have lived this long. During my youth, children were listening to their parent's advice. At least then people tried to follow the rules. But nowadays we are so careless.

FALAGIMUNDALA: There is a change of respect amongst youth and elders. In those days the youth respected parents. But nowadays the young ones talk whatsoever they think is good.

EDES/ TRANSLATOR: He says the young people do whatever they want.

FLORENCE: People are dying each and every time. But in those days, death was scarce. During my youth there was no disease like AIDS. It is a new disease, but it is taking a lot of people. I tell God that if it is possible, that these people should be saved. People are not at peace. There are wars. But during my youth it was not so common. Nowadays people are killing each other everywhere. I live in a world of doubts.

(The elders exit, helping each other to walk, arm in arm. Florence sings, quietly.)

MARGARET: They used to go to the road and sing under the moon for hours, remembering stories from childhood. "And later you part happy," Florence told me. Then Florence sang me a song from her childhood, about being far away from the ones you love. I started to panic. I called my daughter Lucy in Toronto. *(she dials)* Lucy?

LUCY: Mom? Is that you?

MARGARET: I need to talk to someone who knows me.

LUCY: What!!? Mom, you sound weird. Do you have altitude sickness?

MARGARET: No. It's dark. No electricity.

LUCY: At the top of Mount Kilimanjaro?

MARGARET: Things have changed. I'm in this village. I need to make sense of--

LUCY: Mom, slow down. I can't quite hear you.

MARGARET: The car broke down.

LUCY: Are you okay?

MARGARET: Yes. The people are nice.

LUCY: It's good to hear your voice.

MARGARET: I'm listening to the elders. They don't care about the Millennium. You know what its like, another language you don't understand…you start to wonder if you're doing the right thing…

LUCY: Are you sure you're okay?

MARGARET: I'm---Where are you?

LUCY: Deidre took me to this weird party. It's all millionaires.

MARGARET: Millionaires? There must be good food.

LUCY: Is everything okay in Africa? The computers, the power plants—

MARGARET: I don't know …I've been listening to the crickets…. And looking at the sky….

LUCY: Did you say "looking at the sky?"!!!

MARGARET: The fireflies are like flying stars. When you get back we'll do something together. Whatever you want. But right now, Lucy, I need to talk--I've never felt so--

LUCY: Mom, I can barely hear you...I LOVE YOU! HAPPY NEW YEAR! BE CAREFUL.—oops losing the connection...HELLO?! HELLO?(*she hangs up.*)

MARGARET: (*looking at phone, she's hung up.*) I love you too...

(*Lucy is suddenly sandwiched between Suzanne and Joe at the Millionaire's Party in Toronto. They are both very loud and very drunk. Party Music.*)

JOE: The Millennium? Yeah! Its been a huge year for me, I mean I went from being, from...when it was 1998, I was well off, my mom got sick, I got poor real quick supporting my mom, because I took a job with a bad software company that I made no money with, and I went poor real quick and then I was unemployed for four months and then I went real poor, real, real quick and then I took a job with a real good software company, and now I'm a millionaire! SO HAPPY MILLENNIUM!

Some sonofabitch gave me too much champagne REAL TOO EARLY –

LUCY: I didn't get any...where is it? *(Joe blocks her from leaving)*

SUZANNE: I want someone to kiss on the Millennium!

LUCY: Are there any hot guys?

SUZANNE: Plenty.

LUCY: How are you going to choose?

SUZANNE: It's just a matter of...I don't care... I just want someone to kiss on—

JOE: OKAY, YOU CAN KISS A MILLIONAIRE ON NEW YEAR'S EVE AND I'M PROBABLY THE ONLY ONE HERE, SO OKAY—GET WITH THE PROGRAM!

SUZANNE: Yeah, right! *(laughing)*

JOE: HOW ABOUT YOU?

LUCY: I'm only sixteen.

JOE: All the better! *(leans in to kiss her)*

LUCY: No!

SUZANNE: Back off!

LUCY: Yeah!

SUZANNE: Fucking right, man...I thought about this day since I was a little girl. Me and my best friend, we made this pact--

JOE: I made a pact! Its kind of Jim Carreyish but I did it actually. Like ten years ago when I was in high school, well Jim Carrey took it to the extreme...he wrote a check to himself for ten million dollars for acting services rendered...and he actually, well he obviously managed to cash that one...but I wrote a cheque to myself when I was in high school for one million dollars... and that's—

SUZANNE: So you've always been into money, you shallow piece of—

JOE: Shallow piece of shit! *(overlapping)*

SUZANNE: Shallow piece of shit!

JOE: I wrote a cheque to myself for one million dollars—

SUZANNE: I wrote this screenplay which I think is—the fuck knows—

JOE: It's cashable now.

> *(Music Piece; Distorted Countdown. Joe and Suzanne, mutually, drunkenly, decide to kiss. Joe breaks the kiss, almost throws up on Suzanne)*

JOE: I'm not feeling too good.

SUZANNE: *(backing away)* Uh, I gotta go.

JOE: I'm good at making money, but I've never been too good with the ladies.

LUCY: Oh. My. God. Mom? *(tries dialing her cell phone, it doesn't work)* Mom?

(Margaret sitting quietly, staring into space. She is overwhelmed by what the elders have said, and is listening to crickets, watching fireflies....contemplating her life. She sings a Welsh song, softly. Edes (the young translator) is sitting quietly at the edge of the mat. She and Margaret smile at each other. Ricky, a young man in the village, enters and sits on Agogo's chair.)

RICKY: We need money to open a small business, We could pay it back...

MARGARET: Ricky, I don't know.

RICKY: You work for Coca-Cola. Very powerful company. You could bring electricity here.

MARGARET: Ricky, you have something...that people with electricity have lost.

RICKY: What?

MARGARET: There is a sense of belonging, of quiet here. If Coca-Cola moves in, maybe next it will be a strip mall, and Blockbuster Video...I'm sorry, Ricky, that makes no sense to you, does it? I think if Coca-Cola moves in, no-one in your tribe will dance and sing together anymore.

RICKY: It's very difficult to live under the conditions as they are now...a lot of youth turn to what? Armed Robbery. We want a better future. I don't want to be a farmer, like my father.

MARGARET: When I talked to the elders, they said you don't respect them. What do you think, Edes?

(Edes shrugs.)

RICKY: Girls could work for Coca-Cola too.

MARGARET: Edes, why don't you respect the elders?

EDES: We don't respect them. It's not our idea. We are just following. We are just copying it from Western Countries.

MARGARET: Hmm. What kind of education do you get here, Edes?

EDES: Because I am a girl and I am different from the boys here, instead of concentrating on my studies I have a lot of work to do at the house.

RICKY: Oh, Edes! Don't you want a job? Coca-cola to come here? Electricity?

MARGARET: Let her finish.

EDES: If I had a chance of not having so much work to do around the house I could improve at school. Life is different for boys. They can spend time just walking around with nothing to do!

MARGARET: It doesn't have to be that way for girls.

RICKY: About disrespecting our parents. I think it is just time. It's just happening, we didn't copy it from anywhere. Because of the changing of the world we feel at least comfortable to do things we like. But to them we disappoint them. There is no way we can change. If the Malawi government can have negotiations with other countries to attract them to open businesses, they can raise the standard of living for us youth.

EDES: We want a better future than our parents.

MARGARET: I'm sure my daughter feels the same way.

RICKY: Does she want to work for Coca-Cola?

EDES: Maybe we could all work together.

MARGARET: Oh, no, my daughter is going to university-- That would be lovely. Here's my card. We'll talk.

Interlude: AROUND THE WORLD
TASMANIA

(Duet for Actor and Drummer)

BOB *(a Tasmanian Teenager, Australian Accent)*: I don't think the Millennium is important for any religious or scientific reason. I think it's important just because so many people are going to be coming together. It'll be a good party. Everybody else, older people you speak to, they've got something...where were you when Kennedy got shot. I want to say I was doing something exciting in the year 2000. I decided after examining the human race, *(sarcastic)* through deep and rigorous testing, that the main problem with men, in our age, going so spastic and hurting people alot, especially women, was due to lack of guidance and ...uh...role modelling. So I decided I was going to initiate myself somehow. There is this one spot out at my parent's place in the forest I am really scared of....for some reason. Every time I go there I am like "oooooooo" *(spooky sound)*...jittery! *(giggles)* I am going to go out there, camp out, on my own, for a night. Face those fears. My initiation. Maybe I'm hoping for some drastic change in maturity..something like that. Before my 18th birthday. So I'm putting on my tough man boots and hiking out into the woods. We don't get much natural experience in our age.

Scene Twelve: FRANCE

JILL: Emma? Are you all right? *(Emma nods, exhausted. She is huddled on the floor, listening to the radio)*

EMMA: The power is still out.

JOHN: *(entering)* We're back where we belong. The nineteenth century. No light, no phone, no satellite telly. Everything's blissfully pre-industrial, perfectly pleasant, a technophobe's paradise.

(Emma turns up radio. Guitarist amplifies radio through his strings. Actor plays BBC announcer.)

RADIO: This is the BBC World Service. France has been struck by the worst storms since detailed records began in 1660. The storms re-drew much of the French landscape as more than 270 million trees were uprooted in 30 hours. 86 people were killed.

EMMA: The worst storm of the century.

JILL: A natural disaster.

JOHN : An act of god. Maybe Nostradamus was on to something.

RADIO: In Western France, the oil spill of a Total-Fina chartered tanker is expected to kill more seabirds than any previous ecological disaster in the world. On Belle-Ile, the island off the coast of Brittany first hit by the spill, the damage is devastating. As many as 300,000 seabirds have been contaminated. Volunteers are shovelling oil off the sands and rocks. But every tide just brings in more.

(Emma turns radio off.)

JOHN: No act of God this time. An act of man.

EMMA: I've got to get out of here. Off this island!

JOHN: Emma, how can you? There aren't any ferries.

EMMA: I don't know. Charter a helicopter. A water taxi. Anything. I've had enough. I'll leave you to your pre-industrial shangri-la.

JOHN: No. This is ridiculous. It's too dangerous. I'll take you in the morning. Good night! *(exits)*

EMMA: I'm going to the dock and get someone to radio. I'll wait there until I can get off the island.

JILL: It's the middle of the night!

EMMA: I don't care.

JILL: I'm so sorry.

EMMA: Jesus, Jill. It's not your fault. It has nothing to do with you. *(exits)*

(*Music: Transitional Piece. John walks to a "beach area" of the stage. Jill follows.*)

JILL: Here you are. I was worried, so I came looking. The dawn is so beautiful. My God. You can see the oil-- spreading-- in the water.

JOHN: No act of God this time. An act of man.

JILL: John--

JOHN: *(pointing at oil-splattered clothing he is now wearing)* What do you think of my New Year's Eve tuxedo? My *(bad French accent)* "smoking", as the French call it. *(John rubs his gloved finger across the sleeve, producing a sludgy pile of crude oil, which he examines.)* You know, about this much crude oil--*(He holds up a finger covered with oil.)* Something about the size of a twoonie, on the back plumage of a bird, will kill it.

JILL: John, come on!

JOHN: Jesus, Jill, look at it!

JILL: Who are you so angry at? The oil companies? The French? Emma? Me? This is just an excuse. There's 100,000 tons, John. What the fuck can you do about it tonight?

JOHN: Happy New Year, Jillie.

JILL: Do you know it causes cancer?

JOHN: I chainsmoke, for chrissakes.

(John exits. Jill steps forward, kneels touches the oil on the beach. She stands, looking at the oil on her hand. Then she resolves to do something about it, and exits.)

Scene Thirteen: AFRICA

MARGARET: *(at "Africa" window, using chalk on the walls)* All of you already have the skills to empower Africans to start up their own businesses. Here are the key principles you'll be able to use:1. Education--you'll provide training in basic literacy and math skills. 2. Empowerment-- This is the core of the "Kusile," or "New Dawn" program. Many Africans are demoralized. We need to put "I can" into their vocabulary. We are building an African Renaissance.

Remember, if you dream it, we can become it. The youth in Africa want to work, more than any population I have every met. They want to better themselves...through Coca-Cola. Have a break. Anyone want a Coke? They're free, might as well, help yourselves.

Scene Fourteen: NEW YORK

(Siobhan enters, on her beat. It is close to midnight. Tourists are hollering. Nightmare music. She is frightened and paralyzed as the tourists move as if they are experiencing fire in the room, then around themselves, then burn up. Choreography: she turns away, but still tries to reach out. At the end of the nightmare, everyone vanishes and she staggers to a pole, which she leans upon for support.)

MIKE: There you are! I haven't seen you for hours. Our shift's almost over! How's it goin'?

SIOBHAN: Fine.

(Mike has a silver shiny wig. He puts it on and starts dancing.)

SIOBHAN: What the hell are you doing?

MIKE: The tourist association was handing them out. Here, take one.

SIOBHAN: *(she does and holds it awkwardly.)* Oh, Mike.

MIKE: *(waving)* Look, those people from Texas are loving it. They've been trying to get us to loosen up all day.

SIOBHAN: Isn't there anyone here from New York?

MIKE: Nope. Just us 8,000 cops. *(to tourist)* Where are you from?

TOURIST: Iceland!

SIOBHAN: Here! I'm starting to get…agitated…with all these other countries, these other places and times. We're not there. We're in New York which is the heartbeat of the U.S., of the world. Who cares what's happening in Zimbabwe. We should take this wigs off. We could get in trouble with our Lieutenant.

MIKE: It's almost midnight.

(A loud cheer from the dancing tourists. Music fades up. Siobhan begins to panic like it's the end of the world.)

SIOBHAN: You want to have kids? One day.

MIKE: Uh, yeah, sure. One day.

SIOBHAN: I just hope I live to have the chance. You know, Mike, I make fun of you and the other guys, but you did everything right tonight. All of us cops. 100% right.

SFX: Countdown, New York. A Moment of Silence in the Middle. Distorted Sense of Time.

(Siobhan closes her eyes, takes a breath in, wincing. At end of countdown, Mike sets off confetti bottles so that they spray all over them He kisses Siobhan, like in the famous photograph of the soldier kissing the nurse at the end of World War II. They both put on their wigs and start cheering and dancing around.)

MIKE: Look at those idiots.

SIOBHAN: *(laughing)* We're just as bad.

MIKE: O'doul's?

SIOBHAN: Oh, yeah. I think it will be the best beer of my life.

(Music: Transition: Fear Music, Transformed.)

Interlude: SCENES FROM AROUND THE WORLD
CHINA

(Duet for Actor and Cello)

ZHANG: It is real story, and it just happened in the millennium night, at the moment when we were blessing for the bright future All Guangzhou Newspapers have reported this news: When we were joyfully celebrating the millennium, a pregnant woman named Lu Shanhui was being operated for her three broken fingers. Why? She was stealing by the certain supermarket and the guard has her fingers cut. She told the story blubbering, " I prostrate myself at his feet to beg him not to cut, but who knows he really did, and the broken fingers were jumping over on the ground!!" Finally the supermarket was closed by government. . At midnight, fireworks are full of sky. It is real story. Millennium Night. Moment when we were...blessing for bright future.

(Music: Transition into Singapore party, during scene before phone call. Lorraine enters and freezes like a manikin.)

Scene Fifteen: SINGAPORE

BRIDGET: *(at party)* Your New Year's Resolution is to learn my name? Did you know what you do on New Years, you'll be doing all year? Maybe you should hit on someone else. *(into cell)* Lorraine? Is that you?

LORRAINE: How was your dance?

BRIDGET: Good, good. For a while, everyone wanted to talk to me about ancient traditions, the secret lives of women, that sort of thing.

LORRAINE: You always wanted to have a past.

BRIDGET: What do you mean by that? My work is very important to me. So are you. You're very important to me.

LORRAINE: I know. I'm sorry. Are you ever coming home?

BRIDGET: Do you want me to?

LORRAINE: I can't sleep. I barely eat. I don't mind the rain so much when you're here.

BRIDGET: Let's get married.

LORRAINE: What?! Why?

BRIDGET: Because its radical and traditional at the same time. Like us. I love you, Lorraine. I want you to know how much. *(pause)* Are you there?

LORRAINE: Yes. All right. Okay! Yes!

(They burst out laughing.)

BRIDGET: *(Sings "Sweet Lorraine", written in 1928, music by Cliff Burwell, lyrics by Mitchell Parish, weaving in Japanese dance motifs, leading Lorraine into a dance duet that ends in a wedding style kiss.)*

Scene Sixteen: FRANCE

(Cello Music, as in all of France scenes. Other actors place boxes of all sizes and shapes around the stage, as if they all contain birds.)

JOHN: It was bad. When I stood on the cliff, every nook was black, streaked with oil. Jill found a place where we could volunteer to help. I felt so, relieved. Because suddenly we we're being given this chance, because of this horrible tragedy, to feel useful in this world, to finally feel that not everything is for profit. That we can do something.

We went into the hall and everything was silent.

Not a sound, except for the constant tac-tac-tac as air-holes were punched in a mountain of cardboard boxes. Cardboard boxes everywhere, at least a thousand, maybe two. Two minutes later, he comes, like the messiah. Georges. We open our ears. He fills them. Step one: take a box. Step two: cram soup and antibiotics with the probe down the bird's throat -- without damaging its oesophagus. Step three: cram sardines. Four, wash. Five, dry. They are mainly guillemots. And some gannets, which are much much bigger. It takes three people to handle just one. So. First we force-feed the guillemots. Two feedings a day with the probe, and if that works, sardines. If they can't make the transition, if they can't re-learn how to swallow, they'll die. Now it's my turn.

There's a pile of 200 cardboard boxes in front of me. My quota for the night. I take the first box. I can hear the bird inside. I open the box.

(All the actors stand in the area of their main character-- Siobhan, John, Margaret, Bridget. They each open a box. Light spills out from within. Music plays.)

<u>THE END</u>

AFTERWORD

I have been in "art love' with Elaine Avila since she walked into my office at the Women In View Festival in Vancouver in 1988 with a zany comedy about a troupe of actors who are kidnapped by Terrorists in 16th century France. It was very much a first play but I immediately wanted to direct it. It was vividly theatrical with wonderful characters, witty dialogue, and its own unique charm. These qualities are standard in all of Elaine's work and very much present in the four plays in this volume.

For a director and playwright to work well together, there does need to be chemistry, a peculiar kind of meeting of the imaginations of the writer and interpreter. Elaine and I have always had that, and it has resulted in a long and joyous collaboration. I directed the premieres of *Quality, Burn Gloom,* and *Jane Austen Action Figure*, and did a number of workshops for *At Water's Edge*. There is a fluid poetry about these plays that I love and a stylistic openness well suited to a director like myself who is dedicated to non-literal imagery and extended physicality.

As I consider this collection as a body of work, I would coin it a theatre of obsession. Each character is driven by an obsessive need. Roxanne in *Quality* is obsessed with the artistry and status of the very expensive shoes she sells; Pippa is obsessed with Roxanne and her attempt to emulate her idol drives a wedge between them that infuses the frothy comedy of the play with a tinge of sadness. Alice from *At Water's Edge* is obsessed with encasing her marriage in a house that will assure her of perfection, beauty, and security but that relentless quest alienates her husband and she ends up alone. As the house is constructed, the marriage is deconstructed.

This kind of irony is another distinguishing element in Elaine's work. There is a thread of satire at the centre in all she does. It is the kind of satire that is light and funny on the surface but actually uses wit and parody to attack social injustices. *Jane Austen Action Figure* contains a potent commentary on the difficulties women have always faced when they flaunt their independence and travel alone or struggle to integrate love, family and artistic careers. Elaine's female characters are invariably complex; she portrays women as both powerful and vulnerable, and shows us the cost of too much of either. The constant search for self worth is an enduring theme in all four plays.

I retain many memories from my close encounters with the plays here, but I have some favorite moments. *Burn Gloom* was staged in a seedy back room jazz club converted to a glittering environment evoking the spirit of New Year's Eves over centuries and across continents. The small space vibrated with the vivid text of the play and the evocative music contributed by our collaborators, Talking Pictures, an innovative jazz ensemble. There are four powerful monologues in Burn Gloom, sourced from research collected from all over the world on the Millennium New Year's Eve. One day in rehearsal we decided to match each of the four actors performing one of those monologues with a musician and a specific instrument. Each monologue was further defined by the quality of the instruments – cello, trumpet, drums and guitar – and I'll never forget what it was like to hear the results. What evolved was much more than an interesting underscore of text; the actors' voices carried an emotional and psychological rendering of the text and the music added an entirely new layer of meaning. The Grandmother character in Montreal, for example, was able to play optimism and hope for the future while the guitar created her loneliness and vulnerability. With each monologue, the music and text integrated to create something beyond either medium, as if the music was another character, or a reflection of an aspect of the character that would not otherwise have been visible.

Quality was staged in a variety of shoe stores in different cities and each lives in my memory. The first production was at Gravity Pope in Edmonton, a chic shoe store on Whyte Avenue with an amazing selection of beautiful shoes. The actresses and I were able to pick shoes from the store that corresponded to the shoes described in the text, and I felt that the shoes themselves took on the form of new characters in the play. This production was invited to London where we staged the play in a designer shoe store in exclusive Marylebone Lane. We had almost no rehearsal time and at one point the two actresses, Tracy Penner and Melissa Thinglestad, and I were waiting for the store to close so we rehearsed in the ancient alley beside the store, a landmark moment of that entire process. We were working out some physical business for Pippa, examining a moment in the play where she first begins to feel her own power, so there we were in the alley with passersby looking at us oddly as Tracy created an extended physical gesture. I cherish the experience because it captured the nomadic nature of rehearsing *Quality*. We rehearsed in one venue and then mpoved into the store that was always a bit of a foreign space. The store was a commercial site, and we would assume control for a short space of time to run the play, and then it would return to its real function. We were always interlopers, dropping the production onto the space. The tension between the "real" space and the fictional play was one of the most significant points of discourse for the audience in every production of the play.

My favorite recollection from *Jane Austen Action Figure* is running the play for the first time. In the transitions, sheets of writing paper floated down from the catwalk, and an effect I suspected might be heavy handed was magical. The play was staged simply with this as the sole scenic element and it tied the play together thematically and theatrically. Another discovery in this first run was that all of the seemingly disparate individual scenes and the four actors playing many different characters made extraordinary sense and created a series of follow-able arcs —journeys of time, journeys in space, journeys through relationship- that replaced a more conventional single story line, and left the audience feeling satisfied as if they had consumed a full course meal instead of series of snacks.

Jane Austen reflects as well the constant new curiosity Elaine has as an artist. She is not one who settles for what has brought her success but is always on the hunt for a new form, a new theme, a new set of theatrical conventions. I am ever eager to direct the "next" play because it will be a new discovery for her and for me. I look back on these evocative plays that shimmer in my consciousness and look forward to the new work to come.

Kathleen Weiss
December 2011

Elaine Avila's recent works include: *Lieutenant Nun* (based on the true story of a woman conquistador), *Naked Singularity, Step Right Up!, Good Fooling* (inspired by Shakespeare's Clown), *Strike!, Jane Austen, Action Figure, Quality: the Shoe Play, At Water's Edge, Burn Gloom,* and *Made in China*. Her plays have been produced around the world, notably in Central America (Teatro Lagartija, National Theatre of Panamá), New York (Ontological-Hysteric Theatre), France (upcoming), London, England (Tracey Neuls, Nordic Nomad), Edmonton, Alberta (Canadian Centre for Theatre Creation, Gravity Pope, Vault Theatre of Invention, Stage Lab), Vancouver, BC (Cor Departure at Performance Works, Women In View, Lab 1067), Santa Fe, NM (Santa Fe Rep), Albuquerque, NM (Tricklock), Victoria, BC (Theatre SKAM), and Seattle, WA (Theatre Simple). Her favorite collaborations with directors and dramaturgs include: Kathleen Weiss, Ted Gregory, Amiel Gladstone, Karin Coonrod, D.D. Kugler, Joe Peracchio, Rachel Ditor and Heidi Carlsen. She is the recipient of numerous awards including The Victoria Critic's Circle Award for Best

New Play, a Canada Council Millennium Grant, "New Works for Young Women" Award/Residency from Tulsa University, Canada Council/Playwright's Guild of Canada Reading Program Awards, University of New Mexico Large Research Grant (a project with Assistant Professor Mary Anne Santos-Newhall in Lisbon, Portugal), the A.S.K. Theatre Projects Scholarship, Research Fellowship from the Office of the New Mexico State Historian (project on the Harvey Girls) and the Alden B. Dow Fellowship. Her screenplays include "Fortune," "Kai takes a Solo" "Outskirts" "Alvarado" and "Lead Dress" (with Juliet Belmas). She has taught in universities from British Columbia to Tasmania, China to Panamá. MFA: California Institute of the Arts (Suzan-Lori Parks, Erik Ehn, Brian Freeman, Alice Tuan). Publications include: Playwrights Guild of Canada (see website), <u>American Theater</u>, <u>Canadian Theatre Review</u>, <u>Lusitania</u>. She is the Robert Hartung Endowed Chair, Head of the MFA Dramatic Writing Program at the University of New Mexico. Read more at elaineavila.com

NoPassport was founded by playwright Caridad Svich in 2003. It is an unincorporated, artist-driven, grass-roots theatre alliance & press devoted to cross-cultural, Pan-American performance, theory, action, advocacy, and publication.

NoPassport Press Series Editors:
Randy Gener, Mead K. Hunter, Jorge Huerta, Stephen Squibb, Otis Ramsey-Zoe and Caridad Svich

NoPassport is a sponsored project of Fractured Atlas, a non-profit arts service organization. Contributions in behalf of [Caridad Svich & NoPassport] may be made payable to Fractured Atlas and are tax-deductible to the extent permitted by law. For online donations go directly to https://www.fracturedatlas.org/donate/2623.

NoPassport survives purely on individual donations.

For more information about NoPassport please visit

http://www.nopassport.org

Made in the USA
Lexington, KY
05 June 2014